J.S. Breukelaar is an Australian-American author of three novels and one collection of short stories. Her work has won or been nominated for multiple Aurealis and Ditmar Award, the Shirley Jackson Award and others. Her essays and short fiction have appeared in magazines and anthologies worldwide, including *The Dark, Black Static, Fantasy Magazine, Tiny Nightmares: Very Short Stories of Horror*, and several Years' Bests. Her recent publications include the *Bridge* and *Collision: Stories*, and she is currently at work on a new novella among other projects. She lives in Sydney with her family and you can also find her at www.thelivingsuitcase.com and twitter @jsbbreukelaar.

Seb Doubinsky is a bilingual French dystopian writer and poet. He is the author of the "City-States Cycle", comprising, among others, *The Babylonian Trilogy, The Song Of Synth, Missing Signal, The Invisible* and *Paperclip. Missing Signal*, published by Meerkat Press, won the Bronze Foreword Reviews Award in the Best Science-Fiction Novel category in 2018. He lives in Denmark with his family and teaches literature, history and culture in the French department of Aarhus University.

What is being said of *Turning of the Seasons: A Dark Almanac*

"Like a Twenty-first Century Bosch and Bruegel, Breukelaar and Doubinsky conjure nightmare vignettes from the bowels of our most ancient unconscious. Turning of the Seasons is a glorious, grisly folk-horror concept album: Fairport Convention's psychographic ode to Hell."
- J. Ashley-Smith, Shirley Jackson Award winning author of Ariadne, I Love You

"A fantastical book of stories from two unique voices."
- Shirley Jackson Award Winner, Kaaron Warren

"The Turning of the Seasons: A Dark Almanac, by Seb Doubinsky and J. S. Breukelaar, is a compendium of mythic and folkloric short stories and poetry from the realm of the Weird -- a delightfully strange, compact presentation by two fine writers."
- Jeffrey Ford

"J.S. Breukelaar and Sebastien Doubinsky's voices are distinct but marry perfectly in a stripped back fablesque style. They give us delicacy and brutality. They give us *funny*."
- Priya Sharma

Turning of the Seasons

A Dark Almanac

A collection of poetry
and prose by

J. S. Breukelaar
and
Sebastien Doubinsky

Turning of the Seasons: A Dark Almanac

All Rights Reserved

ISBN-13: 978-1-922856-10-4

Copyright ©2022 J.S. Breukelaar & Sebastien Doubinsky

V1.0

All work in this title are original except 'Lifeline', published in Tiny Nightmares: Very Short Tales of Horror, Ed. Lincoln Michel and Nadxieli Nieto, Catapult: New York (2020).

Internal & cover art by Derek Ford, cover design by Greg Chapman. Printed in Palatino Linotype and FreightNeo Pro.

IFWG Publishing International
www.ifwgpublishing.com

Table of Contents

WINTER

Acknowledgements

The authors would like to express their gratitude to all those who have supported them through the years: our agent, Matt Bialer, for *everything*; Gerry Huntman and the team at IFWG Publishing for getting behind our strange project; Priya Sharma, for her kind introduction and for her gorgeous fiction; Jeffrey Ford, for his enthusiasm for *Dark Almanac* and because he is a class act both on and off the page; Derek Ford, for his sublime cover art and illustrations; the Shakey Writers' Workshop for reading early drafts of some of J.S.'s stories; to Seb Doubinsky for dreaming up the *Almanac* and for a dream collaboration; and most of all to our families, for their love and patience.

Introduction

Our understanding of fairy tales is innate. It's not just in our brains, it's in our marrow and our blood. They've been sanitised and infantilised but in their original form they are primal and essential.

J.S. Breukelaar and Sebastien Doubinsky shatter the looking glass and in its shards we see step-mothers, gods, faeries, hunters, shapeshifters, vamp-ires, and witches. Pacts made in dark woods and men-in-black-SUVs. It reflects the not-so-modern maladies of abuse, love (yes, love), loneliness, isolation, imperialism, and war.

This collection has more than its own share of enchantments in shades of Grimm, Faust, Flaubert, and Angela Carter. J.S. Breukelaar and Sebastien Doubinsky's voices are distinct but marry perfectly in a stripped back fablesque style. They give us delicacy and brutality. They give us *funny*.

The Turning of the Seasons: A Dark Almanac is proof that the form will survive and thrive while we have writers like this to reinvent it for us.

Priya Sharma
Wirral, UK
2022

"Last night she came to me, my dead love came in
So softly she came that her feet made no din
As she laid her hand on me and this she did say
'It will not be long, love, 'til our wedding day'"

She Moved Through The Fair, trad.

The Bear, the Witch

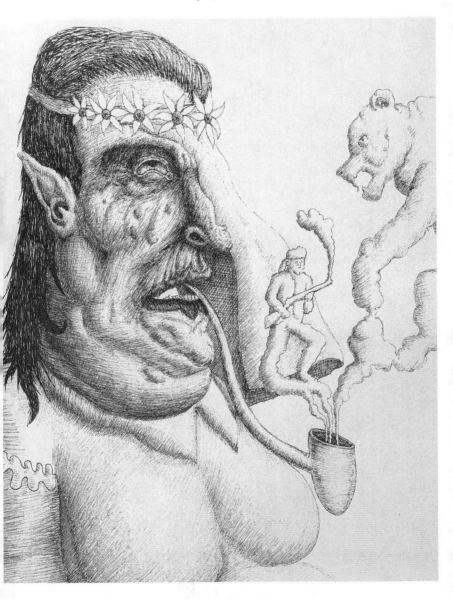

SPRING

The Ring Song

The sun shines like a ring of gold
In the blue sky without a cloud
The sun shines like the wedding ring
My love gave me before dying
The sun sets like a bloody ring
Colour of jealousy and betraying
The sun disappears like a ring of wind
Echoing in hell where his lovers sing

SD

The Bear, the Witch

High in the Hanging Woods lives a huge bear with eyes as blue as ice and fur as white as snow. The bear wakes up one chilly morning with an upset stomach. This is probably due to eating too many fish from the sluggish stream that flows down the grey hills to the edge of the woods. There, in a fetid hut lives an old witch with her pipe and her herbs. The bear decides to visit the witch to see if she can cure its upset stomach. The two go way back to when the bear was a human girl from the village. She'd often liked to stop by the witch's hut for a crust of bread and a sip of milk, or a puff of the witch's aromatic pipe when she wasn't looking. But one day too long ago to even think about, the witch, trying on a new spell, accidentally put a curse on the girl, turning her into a bear. Since then, every year, before the first snowfall, the absent-minded crone guiltily promises herself that by spring, she will have remembered how to undo the curse, but she never does.

First, something for upset stomachs. The white bear snaps and groans while the witch brews a potion of hawthorn and peppermint. But half-way through,

11

perhaps due to puffing too energetically on her pipe, the witch's mind wanders to when she herself was a nymph and not a witch, dancing free through the Hanging Woods. She forgets the recipe for digestive ailments and distractedly tosses in ingredients for insomnia and says some magic words to cure boils, although it is the witch who has the boils, and not the bear.

The Hunter

A black coach with velvet curtains and prancing anxious horses drops the hunter in the valley of the shadow of the dark forest. He ignores his driver's misgivings about strange creatures in the Hanging Woods and how beyond the grey hills is a wild country from which many have never returned. The hunter has trophies on the walls of his library—reindeer and tiger and alligator—but it is the elusive white bear from the Hanging Woods that he seeks. Its head will be the ultimate trophy because a fortune teller of good repute has told him that it will make his young wife love him again.

The hunter is well prepared. He carries a flask of brandy, two loaded pistols, an axe and a long rifle. After a restful night at the one inn in the village, he sets off into the woods. He has not gone far when he comes across a decrepit hut. He knocks on the crumbling door. He calls out that he is looking for the Great White Bear of the Hanging Woods, and seeks directions. The witch invites the handsome hunter in, but makes him promise not to look at her, for she is covered in boils.

The hunter must duck beneath heavy moss dripping from the door of the hut and avert his eyes from the witch draped in a filthy veil from her wedding day. She says she has no knowledge of a white bear, which is close to the truth because the witch still thinks of the bear as a lost child with ice in her eyes and a hunger for warm bread and milk. Instead of information, the witch offers the hunter a twist of dark aromatic tobacco for his pipe.

Enjoying the hag's company more than he wants to admit, the hunter huffs and puffs the fragrant herb. He assures her that he is not mistaken about the bear, for so it was foretold by a fortune teller of some repute. Nevertheless, the smoke makes him a little paranoid, so he asks for a spell to make him lucky in the hunt. The witch names her price. She mixes dried wood-sorrel blossoms and willow root in a beaker of twice-boiled water from the sluggish stream, but midway through she forgets the recipe, and instead drops in some devil's shoestring (which is always unlucky) and recalls scraps of an incantation to invoke kindness, and accidentally confuses it with one for feathers. The hunter drinks the potion which tastes a little fishy. In return he leaves her with two gold coins as arranged, and even throws in his own silver flask—a wedding present—filled with the finest Spanish brandy.

"Your boils aren't bad at all, you know," he says kindly. "I've seen worse."

Soon after penetrating the forest, the hunter steps in bear shit.

"Must be my lucky day," he says a little shakily, recalling how the witch's bridal veil twitched around the in-sucked hole of her mouth. He pulls his boot from the mess. He thinks of his wife, once gay and filled with singing, now grave and silent, at least with him—he has seen her smile furtively at the articles in her magazines or laugh with the servants—and he renews his resolve. The hunter is tall and thin, sad-eyed like his wife, and dark-haired. In spite of the routine drudgery of high finance, not entirely unrelated to the hunt, he sometimes thinks he hears the call of a primordial grace, as if earlier in his life (or in another one) he had been a child of the untamed wood and had bathed in pools bubbling from black rocks draped in glistening vine.

Where there are bear droppings, there must be a bear. And not a small bear, by the look of it, but a bear worthy of pursuit—perhaps the Great White Bear of presage? The hunter stops between the trees beside the still stream. He kneels down and presses his fine hand within the clumsy outlines of a lumbering paw print. The size confounds him. His flesh crawls with anticipation. A prize to be sure. He imagines his wife's lovely dark eyes widening—so wide perhaps that he will find himself in them again—when he comes home to present her with the glistening white head.

He is glad of his axe.

The hunter gets to his feet and sniffs the air. There is a pile of rank droppings near the paw print, and he sniffs that too. He wrinkles his brow. It is the smell of an animal not right in itself. It is the reek of disease.

Of death. As if on cue, a vulture alights on a branch further on. It angles its bald head at the hunter and furls its wings like a cloak. A feather floats to the ground. The witch's fragrant high has worn off and the hunter's heart sinks. The bear is on its last legs. A sick bear, presaged or not, is no contest.

And yet he must go on to the end. It was foretold, even if there is a new foe now, a late entrant in the race: Death itself. The hunter must get to the bear before It does. Wily nemesis—he sees that now. Death was never his servant, never his ally. Always his foe. Waiting for a chance to beat him to the hunt. The hunter grimaces. The contest is changed but it is still a contest.

I am the champion, he thinks. Hear me roar.

He peers just once down the barrel of his rifle for luck, and creeps on, following the scent of the bear droppings. When he emerges finally on stony ground above the stream, the leaves are all gone from the trees and the sun has begun its descent. He follows the footprints through the grey speckled stones for a long, long way.

The Bear

The beautiful white bear is unable to keep as far ahead of the hunter as she would like. Her stomach is really upset. She never really took to being a bear—she misses the comfort of fresh bread, warm milk and a purloined pipe. She tries not to think about what it was like to be a girl and scramble beside the stream to the high moonlit ridge with the standing stones and leafless trees and beyond that even further, a cave with a brimming pool among the glistening moss—a secret place where there was no one to see her unbutton her dress and take off her shoes and stockings. No one to see her go down into the water, which was warm and soft as fingers, soft as a kiss.

The bear lumbers along, stopping every now and then to squat painfully in the bushes. Her majestic white rump is streaked with brown, matted with thistle and twigs. The witch's potion is not as effective as it should have been, and she had been a fool to trust her again.

The Hunter

The vulture unfurls its wings and flaps to the next tree. The musk of sick bear is almost intolerable. The hunter takes strength thinking of its snarling head frozen for all eternity above his fireplace, and in the flames from the setting sun, he sees the firelight burn in his wife's laughing eyes. He is the hunter and the prey has changed. It is now Death itself that he seeks, and he will wrestle the bear's head from the fickle sickle of time. The vulture, Death's own messenger, has thrown down the gauntlet.

He wishes he hadn't left his flask with the witch. The temperature is dropping fast and the light is draining from the sky. He is glad he is wearing his fur jacket. He can no longer see the valley below. The great stones loom ahead, washed red as blood. The vulture is a speck on a bough in the distance, leading him ever onwards. Finally, he comes to the hanging woods and the hunter begins to climb. The sun is a low glow on the horizon and he can barely put one foot in front of the other.

He comes to an escarpment—its black walls all but eclipse the crimson rays of the sun. Shadows play behind the canted limbs of the trees and in the dimness he sees what he came for. A cave gouged out of the black rock. The hunter knows a bear cave when he sees one. He follows the deep maundering prints into the shadows and up a steep path carved out by a beast bigger than any he has encountered before, if the broken branches are anything to go by. Berries have been torn off the thorny bushes that block the mouth of the cave. The hunter approaches silently. He calculates the distance to the valley where the carriage will collect him—a long way to drag a bear's head, and he hopes he will be able to follow the trail in the dark. The vulture alights on the top of the escarpment, its plumage ill-fitting as a gravedigger's. With glee the hunter acknowledges the low snarls coming from inside the cave. The bear is still alive!

The hunter knows what he's doing. He creeps soundlessly as close to the mouth of the cave as he dares, counting on the bear to catch his scent despite its illness. He fires a pistol into the air to draw the bear out. And quickly shoulders his rifle.

As expected, the white bear lumbers out on all fours, its muzzle raised to the scent, and its dazzling pelt streaked with filth. It roars and stands up, the height of two men, and the hunter is close enough to be almost as surprised at its size as the fact that

17

it's female, and to recoil at her musk. His rifle shot goes wide, nicking the bear on the shoulder and filling her with rage. She is on the hunter in a hot second. The look of surprise is frozen on his face as she rips off his head, tossing his body into the shit-strewn foliage.

The Girl, the Witch

The bear drops back to all fours and rolls the hunter's head inside the cave. Snow is in the air, and it is time to leave the year behind her and look to the next one. To sleep on it, as an absent-minded witch once said, because everything looks clearer in the morning. The vulture drops soundlessly from the branch and begins to feast.

The bear sleeps.

After a long, long time, the snow melts and a woman emerges naked from the cave. Her eyes are as blue as ice and her long white hair falls down to her feet, and in her hand she carries a human skull. She has a puckered scar on one shoulder.

Down in the valley in a mouldering hut, the witch wakes from a dream of picking wildflowers in the Hanging Woods. She smiles and removes her veil. Her boils are gone, and even better, she has finally remembered what was needed to reverse the curse of the white bear—a hunter's bullet of course! And not just any hunter but one whose skull will make a handsome candleholder, and in spring a pretty pot in which to plant the fragrant leaf for her pipe. She cuts some thick slices of freshly baked bread and pours milk to heat at the stove for her long-awaited visitor. Better late than never, she thinks, feeling quite pleased with herself.

JSB

Prayer Fragment

My head rests upon the red moon
While stars crackle around the hips of the
  sky
We dream together of water and wind
Your right hand holding my heart
Your left one caressing my antlers
While you whisper a wish and a curse

SD

The Innocent Child

One day, the goddesses and the gods decided to have a party in their palace high on top of the sacred mountain. They ate and drank and listened to beautiful music and admired the delicate dancers and astounding acrobats. Later in the evening—or it might have been early in the morning—they decided to have a friendly contest to decide who was the most powerful of them all. The winner would have the right to rule over all the others for a full day and a full night.

"I am the most powerful," said the Sun Goddess, her immense beauty warming up all the other divine faces. "There would be no day without me, and the world would smother in the darkness."

"No, it's me!" said the Night God, shrouding all with his dark velvet cape. "Without me, nobody could sleep and dream about a better life."

All the gods and goddesses stood up one after the other, claiming the title. Finally, a small child walked into the room, a frail little girl who bore the touching and eerie crooked smile of the eternally innocent. She wore a dirty little white dress and faded roses crowned her hair.

"What are you doing?" she asked. "Can I play too?"

"Oh, we are not playing anything," the Sun Goddess hurried to say.

"We are just having a grown-up discussion, that's all," the Night God lied, because the imbecile child was the Goddess of Death.

She was without a doubt the most powerful of them all and they were all terrified of what she could do if she ever won the contest.

SD

Avian Medicine

My woman is Queen of the Faeries. When she was a girl people were always trying to clip her wings. By the time she finally finds me she has forgotten how to fly. So I show her how to give the budgies their drops, dress the wounds of a crow, fill feeders with birdseed. She goes away sometimes, and the other men think she belongs to them but I know the truth—that whoever will be the next King of the Faeries, it is the one who can fix a broken bird.

JSB

Friedlichstadt

I remember looking up the name on Google translate. 'Peaceful town' it said. I liked that. Exactly what I was looking for, if the name matched the city. I had been on the road for a long time, doing some location scouting for my next documentary, which would be about ghost legends in northern Germany and Scandinavia. I was on my way to Denmark, driving from Hamburg, where I had visited a couple of places, including a brothel on the Reeperbahn, which was rumoured for the sighting of the ghost of a murdered prostitute—but that's another story.

There was no ghost story attached to Friedlichstadt, at least nothing I could find, and I thought it would be a welcome break from my week-long tour, before moving on. If the city was as pretty as the pictures posted on the Internet, it would be a great place to relax for a day.

I arrived early Saturday afternoon, and the place was, indeed, as charming as the pictures I had seen. The streets were narrow and cobbled, but as all the houses were painted white and the doors different colours, there was nothing sinister about it. A few hollyhocks sprung here and there from between the stones, adding a charming note to the tableau. I parked my car on the main square, which hosted the old town hall, a large café which also served as restaurant, and my hotel. All were 18th century buildings, with discreet stucco decorations of flower garlands and cherub faces.

I checked into my hotel. The lady behind the counter in the lobby didn't speak English very well, but we laughed together at my terrible German as she finally delivered me the key, pointing at the number on the attached copper tag. Climbing a narrow and creaky wooden staircase smelling of beeswax, I carried my bags in my room, which was large and comfortable. After a quick and relaxing shower, I decided to take a walk around those charming streets.

Spring was in full bloom and the air was charged with the lazy warmth of the young sun. A faint breeze flattered my cheeks while I crossed passers-by strolling along, coming in and out of shops, chatting in German and laughing. I visited a few stores, bought a scarf for my wife and an excellent pastry for myself. I walked along the narrow river that cut the town in half, looked at my reflection while stooping from the charming wooden bridge, enjoying my spare time.

I finally arrived at the church, a large white-washed 14th century building. At least, that's what it said on the bronze sign next to the large wooden double-door. Although I couldn't read German, the dates were obvious to me. It had a high spire, which soared from its facade like a pointy lighthouse, but the rest of the building was surprisingly simple, like a shoebox made of bricks painted white. There were, however, large arched windows on its sides, but without any stained glass. Just dull, boring dusty glass geometrically divided into small greyish lozenges connected by welded lines of ancient lead. I tried to open the doors—both the front one and a side one—but to no avail. They were locked. I thought maybe they would be open on Sunday morning for mass, but I would be on my way to Denmark by then.

The sun was descending as I walked back in the direction of my hotel, and I realized my stomach was grumbling. I stopped at the café, where I had a fairly decent meal, after once again having to struggle to make myself understood. The menu was also only in German, which didn't simplify things.

Going back to my hotel, which was on the other side of the square, I couldn't refrain an ironic smile thinking about how many saw English as the lingua franca in the world. I thought we were still a long way from the power of Latin. Maybe for the better, actually. Who needed crazy emperors and bloody circus games, except for the money-grabbing medias?

Before climbing up the squeaky stairs to my room, I grabbed a tourist leaflet from a pile I hadn't noticed when I had signed in. I exchanged a polite smile with the woman behind the counter—the same as in the morning—and hurried up, afraid to get into a much confusing and helpless conversation again.

After setting up my laptop on the little desk provided in the room, I took a quick glance at the leaflet I had brought up with me. Friedlichstadt seemed to have an interesting history, or rather an interesting lack of. Originally founded by an archbishop in 1136, it was a small city of no importance and seemed to have remained so through the ages. There was no record of invasions or destruction, even during world war two. Nobody famous was ever born there. One particularity, noted in the leaflet, was that they weren't any military memorials, as the town's men miraculously all seemed to have survived the numerous wars that had plagued Europe. Its few Jews had also escaped the terrible fate of the rest of their community. Its name meant 'peaceful town' and it had even received a UNESCO award for its specificity.

I felt like running down the steps and asking the receptionist all sorts of questions, but our limited communication seemed like an insurmountable obstacle. I decided to work on my notes, and so I did, soon forgetting all about the leaflet and the historically incredibly insignificant town I had come to.

When I felt I was finished, I shut my computer down and looked at my watch. It was a little over ten, the perfect time for a good beer before going to bed. I was in Germany after all, and this was a country famous for its variety of local brands. Maybe Friedlichstadt had its own special pilsner and I was eager to discover what it tasted like.

The lady behind the counter had vanished, and

I made sure I had the key in case I returned late. I stepped outside, planning to get a beer at the café on the other side of the square but, to my surprise, it was already closed. I was taken aback a little as though Friedlichstadt had not appeared to me a busy town, it was the weekend and there should have been at least a couple people as thirsty as me.

I looked around, but not a soul was in sight. I began wandering the narrow streets behind the town hall, only hearing my own steps on the irregular cobblestones. A strange feeling began to seep into my soul, as if something was not quite right, but I couldn't put my finger on it. I realized what it was when I stopped in front of the large window of the souvenir shop: apart from the feeble streetlights, not a single window was lit. The whole town was either already sleeping, or it was just a huge film set, abandoned for the night. I resumed my search for an open bar or café, looking up and down to find some form of life, but in vain. The town was dead. Completely dead.

I decided to turn around and get back to the safety of my hotel, when I heard a strange sound — or rather, a strange melody. It sounded as if it was played on a transverse flute, low and haunting, neither sad nor happy. Surprised, I stopped, trying to localize its source — I was thinking that there might be a concert somewhere, which would have explained where all the people were. I began to follow the notes, although I couldn't really place where they were coming from. It alternatively sounded louder or weaker, but not in a coherent fashion. It sounded like a Debussy piece, something like *Prélude à l'après-midi d'un faune*, but I knew my Debussy, and this wasn't by him.

After having turned a few corners, I arrived in front of the church. There seemed to be some light glowing through the stained-glass windows and I approached, thinking that the mystery would be solved soon. There was a concert taking place. Laughing at myself and my previous anguish, I tried to discreetly open the front door first, which was locked. I walked up to the side door, but it was locked too. The music had stopped now and the silence that filled the square had become almost palpable, like an ominous presence. I am generally not superstitious although I make documentaries about ghosts and occult things, but I suddenly felt very oppressed, breathing for air as if I was suffering an asthma crisis.

As I hurried back to my hotel, half in a panic and half laughing at myself, I suddenly bumped into a stranger I hadn't seen coming. Our shoulders made violent contact and I fell on my ass, letting out a short cry of pain. The stranger looked at me and I gasped. His eyes were pale and silver, with a flatness that reminded me of old coins that had been rubbed too many times. He lifted a finger to his mouth, and said, "shhhhhh!". I nodded and got up to my feet, glad to have found a living being, even if his eyes were very eerie. Maybe he was blind, I thought—which would explain our collision.

"Do you speak English?" I asked him. "Do you know where I could find—"

"Shhhhh!" the man said again, with the same

gesture, which was more a command than a polite enticement. His other hand grabbed my shoulder and forced me closer to his face.

"This is a quiet town," he said in perfect English. "You go back to your bed now. Do not disturb the peace here. We don't like to be disturbed."

His fingers dug deep in my shoulder, making me wince. Before I could react, he had pushed me back against the wall and disappeared in the shadows. My shoulder felt hot, as if it had an infection.

When I finally got back to my room, half-running all the way, to be honest, I took a look at my skin in the bathroom. There were bruises alright, but they didn't look like finger marks. They looked as if someone had bitten me with huge teeth. Some blood was even seeping through the abominable wounds.

I couldn't sleep the rest of the night, waking up every half hour in sweat and plagued with terrible nightmares. I decided to leave at the first rays of dawn, planning on leaving cash for the room at the reception desk, but when I landed at the bottom of the stairs with my luggage, the usual woman was there, fresh and smiling. I handed her my card without saying a word, signed the receipt and left as fast as I could.

Later, much later, when I reached my hotel in Copenhagen, before taking a much-desired shower, I checked my shoulder in the bathroom mirror. Even if it was still hurting, the bruises had almost disappeared, and the blood had dried and scabs had fallen off, leaving a couple of barely visible whitish half-moons. What a crazy story, I thought, beginning to doubt what I had just experienced.

After a wonderfully warm shower, I decided to Google Friedlichstadt again, thinking that I should do more research about this town, with the idea of taking a film crew there for a documentary. I could do a 'real life' documentary, maybe asking other people through my website to come up with their own weird experiences of the city.

Google suggested Friedrichstadt, but that wasn't the name of the city I had just visited. I typed the name again, thinking I might have misspelled it. The same answer came up. There was no Friedlichstadt to be found. I checked Google maps, Google pictures, Google videos. Nothing. No Friedlichstadt, only Friedrichstadt.

As I reclined in the uncomfortable armchair of the hotel, my head buzzing with all sorts of contradictory thoughts, I remembered I had paid my hotel room with my Visa card. I logged into my bank account, but no transaction appeared. Shaking my head, I began to laugh. I laughed and laughed until my eyes were wet with tears, but I didn't wipe them off: at least they were undeniably real, and I wasn't crazy. I wasn't crazy. I wasn't crazy.

SD

Eye For An Eye

When everyone in the village accused her son of having the evil eye—how even a brief glance from her him would bring on the death of a cow, an attack of killer bees, a lover's betrayal—Eileen took action. Taking a clean kitchen cloth from the drawer, she blindfolded Luke to prove that his pallid stare had nothing to do with their bad luck or bad choices, that the universe no more whispered its ill intent into his ears than into any others. The problem was that soon after the blindfold was on, the bad things in the village stopped happening. The harvest was good and the milk was sweet and lovers frolicked behind every blossoming tree.

A posse formed to see to the lad.

Eileen rode at dusk to the castle on the hill to beseech the Lord within who'd forced himself on her, to save his bastard son, for surely the lynch mob would take away her only child. The Lord would not receive her and one of his guards gave her a fat lip for her trouble. The sun was a line of crimson on the horizon. As she limped away across the drawbridge, she chanced to look over her shoulder up at the castle windows and was gripped by a sense of the solid ground falling away from her. The curtain of her Lord's bedchamber was drawn aside, two eyes of burning flame glared down from the formless shadows.

Eventually, summoning motion to her limbs, Eileen untethered the mule and rode home, barring the door behind her. She put a poker to redden in the fire and sat down to wait. But the expected posse never came. Her son sat patiently in his room with his blindfold on. Just before dawn, she ventured out the front door and, stumbling on a milk bucket left on her path, emerged into the square. There was not a human soul in sight. The houses were shuttered and empty. The windows of the apothecary and general store were coated in dust. Lichen bloomed in the churchyard across the square.

The rattle of the milk bucket in the silence alerted her to the boy who'd followed her out. He put a hand on her shoulder, still with his blindfold on. She turned around and took it off.

"Did you do this?" she said. "You really did have the Eye?"

He nodded. "But not anymore."

"Where are they now?"

He shook his head. "In a dark place."

"Can you see me?"

He shook his head. "Not anymore."

He'd bargained with the only thing he'd inherited from his father, his Sight. And it cost him dearly. He did it for me, Eileen thought, for us.

"Get the people back," she said. "They won't bother us again."

"Then can we go to father's castle like you always promised?"

"Your father's dead," she said, which is what she should have told him in the first place. Sometime a lie is closer to the truth than the facts.

Eileen led her son back into the house—he remembered where the milk bucket was and picked it up so she wouldn't trip on it again. When the villagers returned, they all scratched their heads at having had the same dream. But they were different, not only because it wasn't an ordinary dream, but also because they intuited that it came at great cost to the dreamer. Perhaps it was for this reason that never a day passed without a basket of bread, a brace of pheasant or sack of apples left on the doorstep of the widow and her poor blind son. It didn't matter why, they reasoned to themselves, it just seemed like the right thing to do.

The boy grew tall and straight and bonny, and married a kitchen maid from the great castle, as beautiful on the outside as she was within.

JSB

212

March sucked. It was cold, wet and freezing and schooldays felt like they would never end. After the electric buzzing of the bell and amidst the rumble of 25 pupils jumping from their chairs, I picked up my textbooks and stuff and met in the yard with my pals Jerry, Paulie and Chris, who were impatiently waiting for me.

"You like school so much you want to stay a little bit longer?" Jerry asked, his freckles dancing on his nose as he grinned.

"Come on," Paulie said. "You know he's slow. He's just slow."

Chris said nothing, just stared at me as he always did with his sad eyes, as if the others' remarks personally hurt him.

"Don't forget to do your homework, Jerry! You're on tomorrow morning! Math problem!" Mister Benz shouted after us as we hurried down the long corridor.

"Fuck him and fuck him twice and sideways," Jerry muttered under his breath and we all laughed at the bad words.

Jerry knew so many of them, because his older

brother used them all the time. And he smoked too. And didn't care. We all worshiped his older brother. A God to us all, and some of his Divinity had befallen upon his little brother. At least, in our circle. Mr. Heinz was much less convinced.

The darkened streets welcomed us like a vampire wrapping us in his cape. This was the time when my heart felt squeezed underneath my ribs and a queasy sadness filled me. I knew it must have been because of my mother's death. She had withered away during the winter three years ago and she had been buried in the beginning of spring. Every March I missed her more than usual, because of the memories.

My father had taken in a tenant—Miss Flannery. She stayed in the empty room next to my father's, which used to be my mother's studio. I know they had met in the advertisement agency they both worked at and that she badly needed a place to stay. My father asked me if that was okay and I had said "yes". Sometimes I wonder what would have happened if I had said no, but like my father always said, "things are as they are, and that's the way things are."

We walked fast until we reached the middle of the street, where number 212 occupied its sinister spot.

"The Bad House! The Bad House!"

Jerry pretended to scream like a girl and we all laughed. Paul made faces like a demon, Chris howled in pain and I laughed like a mad scientist. Although we were laughing, I knew that we all felt a little scared of the large dark building that stood in the middle of the street. The Bad House had a reputation in the city—and even beyond. Half a century earlier, it had been the scene of some horrible things. Our parents didn't want to tell us what had happened there, but we knew it had involved children—and I guess that was all we actually wanted to know. Rumour was that the house had never been sold. It still stood there, three stories high of emptiness, with its locked shutters and door. Twice a day we passed in front of it, going to and coming back from school. Twice a day we were a little bit scared.

"Aren't you going to ring the bell?" Jerry said to me.

I shrugged and he pushed me, laughing. With his half-long blonde hair, blue eyes and freckles, he was the handsomest of us all—and the most precocious too, thanks to his older brother. Paulie, a slightly overweight boy with curly hair and divorcing parents, grabbed a scoop of frozen snow from a car top and crushed it against Chris's neck, who screamed and tried to kick him. Chris was the smallest in our group, a year younger than us, but so bright he had moved up one class, where he slaughtered us all in mathematics and geography.

We were at the bottom of the steps that led to the door of the Bad House now.

"Aren't you going to ring the bell?" Jerry asked again.

The old joke. Every time we passed in front of the sinister building either one of us would challenge another to ring that bell. Until now, no one had ever dared to do it—earning every time the "chicken" adjective and the sneers of the others. Normally, I would have just accepted my fate and moved on, but that day was slightly different. That morning, at breakfast, I had learned that my father was going to marry Miss Flannery, and that I should call her Frances. If I liked Miss Flannery very much, I still felt loyal to my mother and although I nodded and accepted to be hugged by each one in their turn, something had shut in me and I had decided it was a bad day. A mediocre grade for my last math test had confirmed that, as well as the fact that Judy hadn't been at school today. Judy was the new girl, a pretty brunette with blue eyes that made my heart freeze and crack every time she lay them on me— which was, unfortunately, not very often.

Chris was beating up Paulie now, of course, being one year older, twice his weight and several inches taller. I stared at them while Jerry was still nagging me. The image of my father, looking so serious this morning, Miss Flannery a few steps behind him, as if already his shadow, lay like a film before my eyes, tainting everything. I thought about the only picture of my mother that I had, standing on my desk in its silver frame. A beautiful woman, with a nice smile and tender black eyes. Her hair was as blonde as Miss Flannery's was black. I felt angry at my father, I felt angry at Jerry, I felt angry at the world.

"No problem," I said. "I'll do it."

Jerry stared at me as I put my hand on the rusty

black railing. His mouth opened, then shut. Seeing my hesitation, his surprised expression morphed into a sneer.

"Oh yeah?" he said. "I'd like to see that, chicken man."

"Don't call me chicken man. I said I'll do it."

Paul and Chris stopped their fighting and joined Jerry. All were silent, but their eyes were watching me closely.

I climbed the first three steps and turned around. Seeing my three friends standing in awe made me smile and I waved at them. Chris was the only one to lift his hand. Turning around, I resumed my expedition until I reached the eighth step. A sudden gust of cold wind slapped me in the face and I almost fell backwards.

"Wow!" I said. "Did you feel that?"

"Feel what?" Jerry said.

"Never mind," I said.

I stared at the 212 nailed above the door. Made of copper that had lost its shine a long time ago, the numerals looked like ancient weapons stuck in the wall. I shivered and turned my attention to the doorbell. It was an antique electrical device, round with a small button in the middle. No name above or under it. Just a plain and simple, boring doorbell. I glanced one last time at my comrades before I quickly pressed the button. Feeling triumphant, I hurried down the stairs, expecting cheers and greetings, but my friends just looked at me suspiciously. "You're still a chicken," Jerry said. "You didn't really press the doorbell."

I couldn't believe my ears.

"Yes, I did! I just did!"

"Couldn't see anything from here," Paul said, shaking his curls.

"It's because it's getting dark," Chris explained, always the rational one. "You have to press longer, so we can see it."

I hesitated. I knew I had pressed the doorbell and I had felt mighty courageous. But what was it worth if those idiots hadn't seen me do it? What could be worse than be called a "chicken" when you knew you were a hero—but were the only one?

I climbed back up the stairs and pressed the button with all my strength again, leaving it on so that the others could see this time. I looked at them, more guessing their presence than seeing them, as Chris had been right. It was quite dark now. The streetlights would be turned on any minute now. I finally let my finger off the bell and turned around out to scram out down the steps again.

Behind me, the door went 'clunck!'

Startled, I looked behind my shoulder and saw the door was slightly opened.

"Okay, we seen it!" Chris cried.

"Yeah! Let's go! I'm freezing", Jerry added.

Drawn between fear and curiosity, I saw myself reach for the massive bronze doorknob and push it slowly. I moved slightly forward, holding my breath, amazed at my own courage. The last thing I heard was Paul's voice, urging me to come down. Then something like a gust of wind pushed me inside and the door slammed shut behind me.

I was still outside, on top of the stairs, but it was morning, or so it seemed. I was staring at the closed door, with its round doorbell and the half-rusted 212 staring back at me. In shock, I tried to open the door again, but it was locked. I pressed the doorbell again and again, to no avail. My eyes filled up with tears, but I swallowed them back. I had done it, after all. I had pressed the doorbell. Even Jerry hadn't dared! No more "chicken" for the rest of my life, that was for sure!

I bravely walked down the steps in the half-day-light. The street was empty, which was strange, and covered in a fine light-gray dust, which was even stranger. No more snow, and it actually felt a little warm, so I took my other glove off and opened my duffle-coat. Silence reigned. And that was spooky.

Disoriented, I looked around. This was the street that I knew, that I took every day to go to school, the street where Paul, Chris and Jerry and I lived, a few numbers away from each other. And that was the movie theatre in front of which we met every day, a little farther down, right after the barber shop where I got my hair cut every month or so, when my father remembered. Yes, that was definitely the street and yet I was looking at it with a strange feeling of queasiness. Then it hit me: the street was in reverse. All the shops were in the wrong order, or rather—in the reverse order. The school was not on the right anymore, but on the left. The movie theatre, on the contrary, was on the right. I ran up the steps of the Bad House again, this time in panic, trying to turn the doorknob and frantically pressing the doorbell. Tears ran down my cheeks and this time I didn't care and let them flow freely. I wanted to go home and I didn't care if my father was going to marry Miss Flannery. I didn't care at all!

I stopped, sobbing. My hands and clothes were covered in that powdery grey dust now, which seemed to be carried by an invisible breeze. I walked down the steps and stopped, not knowing what to do. That's when I noticed that strange objects were scattered around, half-covered by dust. There was a long one at my feet and I crouched to look at it. It was a bone. I didn't know if it was human, but it was long and white. Lifting my eyes, I saw a round one, a few feet away. When I came closer, I saw it was a skull, and by the size of it, of a child, probably my age. There were bones everywhere, of all sizes. They lay on the pavement, in the middle of the asphalt, in the gutter. The warmth was growing too. I grew scared. I walked over to the coffee shop across from the house, hoping that someone might be working—even if it was early in the morning, maybe someone was cleaning up or something. I peered through the film of dust but saw no one. I tried to push the door, but it wouldn't move. I could see there were more bones inside.

A tremor ran through my legs, as if a small earthquake was shaking the town. We didn't live in an earthquake zone—I knew that much from my geography classes. It stopped and started again. And again. Then I heard it. A low rumble, like a peal of thunder, when it is far, far way. I looked at the sky above the buildings, but it was still that strange dawn blue. Not a cloud. I walked to the middle of the street. The tremors continued, a little harder now and the noise was clearer. It reminded me of the steps of the giant in Jack and the Beanstalk. It sounded loud and terrifying and it was coming my way.

I scanned the street, looking for somewhere to hide. I tried a few more doors, but they were all locked. The sound grew louder, closer. I had to hide, I had to flee, I had to run. I thought of my father, of Miss Flannery, of my mother, of all my friends, of all the people I wanted to see again. Yes, even Miss Flannery, even if I actually hated her with all my heart and wished my mother had never died. Miss Flannery was a paper cut-out, with no flavour nor charm. But still—at that moment, I would have loved to see her too.

Home.

Yes, maybe that was the way.

Home.

I had to try.

I ran in the opposite direction of my normal home. The bones were bouncing up because of the tremor and the sound was so loud I couldn't hear myself think. My lungs were filled with fire and my legs seemed to be made of steel as I sprinted towards my father's house. Jerry's house. The movie theatre. Chris' house. The bakery. Paul's house on the other side. The ground began shaking under my feet. My house. My house!

I ran up the three steps and looked for the key

in my pocket. My fingers were trembling and tears blurred my eyes. I managed to set the key into the lock and turn it, pissing a little in my pants as the sound became deafening. The door opened. I was home.

I slammed the door behind me and I let myself slide onto the floor. As my breath slowed, I realized the ground wasn't shaking any more. I listened. The noise was gone. Or rather, it had been replaced by another noise. The noise of traffic. I slowly raised myself up and looked through the peephole. February was back, the streetlights were on, and the traffic hummed normally at the crossroad. I could see the silhouettes of the passers-by hurrying home, with the white puff of their breaths preceding them.

Still shaking, I lay my school bag at the bottom of our stairs and walked towards the kitchen, trying to ignore the dark smelly stain decorating the front of my pants. I pushed the door open and saw Miss Flannery's back, as she was washing something in the sink. I noticed she had a new dress on, a light blue one I had never seen before, and that she had dyed her hair blonde. Then she turned around to greet me and something shattered in me, like a mirror falling on the ground.

"What's the matter, darling?" My mother said. "You look like you've just seen a ghost."

SD

The Collector

The white man walked into my house, escorted by a soldier in a dirty uniform, a rifle on his back. I could smell the mixed odour of their stale sweat before they pushed the curtain aside hanging in front of the entrance to my hut. I had heard my two servants try to shoo them away, but to no avail. The man had an interpreter with him, but I told him I didn't need one—I spoke the language of the foreign rulers. The man was quite young, but looked tired and had yellowish skin—maybe the consequence of a fever.

"You are the priest of this village, yes?" he asked me.

I nodded, although the word 'priest' in his language didn't mean much in ours. I was more of a guardian—of memories, of rites, of traditions that came before our grandfathers' fathers.

"A woman," he added, stating the obvious.

I nodded again. What else could I say?

"I come to buy some objects," he said. "I will take them to my country, with good care. I am a collector. I am very interested in your culture."

I had no idea what a "collector" was, so I said

nothing, sitting on my little stool.

"I have money," he resumed, taking a wad of bills from the pocket of his sweat-stained cotton jacket.

I smiled. Money was always good.

"Can I look around?"

The soldier looked at me threateningly. He was from the south, with no respect for our customs. Our ancient enemies, now the army of the new white rulers. We were a great empire too, ages ago, and they were our slaves. The irony of history.

"Of course," I said, as if I had a choice.

He scanned the room, squinting in the half darkness. He told the soldier to bring him two masks and a sculpture of Gun, our god of iron and war. The soldier took them and placed them at his feet. He rubbed his chin, nodding. His eyes then caught sight of the Nameless One in the corner, covered with an old fabric embroidered with silver and gold. He gestured to the soldier to go and lift the fabric, but I raised my hand to stop him.

"No," I said. "Not that one."

The soldier grabbed his gun, but that didn't frighten me. The Nameless One frightened me more than him. The story was that a woman had come with the statue, after we had conquered her nation. She was to marry the king. She brought the Nameless One with her as a present, and it was a curse: our king died young, his sons were all killed in battle, and we lost everything. Our empire, our wealth, our power. When the foreigners came, all they had to do is plant their blue, white and red flag, and that was it. All our power was gone.

The soldier moved towards the Nameless One, and I tried to grab his thigh, but he kicked me from my stool. He lifted the fabric and the Nameless One appeared, magnificent and ominous, standing in the corner of my hut.

The white man walked passed me, actually over me, not giving me a glance. He looked transfixed by the statue.

"I want this," he said, turning to me.

I was sitting on my stool again, my old bones aching from the fall.

"No," I said. "It's bad luck. Very bad luck for your country. It brings war. It brings destruction."

The white man laughed.

"We're in 1913, dear madam, and I am not superstitious!"

He told the soldier to take it, and threw a wad of bills at my feet.

I didn't pick it up, but followed them outside. They walked to their truck, with another soldier behind the wheel. The white man opened the back of the truck, and the soldier shoved in the two masks, Gun and the Nameless One before climbing in his turn.

As the vehicle disappeared in a cloud of yellow dust, I silently sent a prayer to the Nameless One, bidding it farewell, a safe trip and not to forget its duty as the Spirit of Revenge.

SD

A Wild Dog

SUMMER

Taz

When the creature growled at the pinewood slats of its cage—maybe it was the splinters or sumthing, I said—Harley rummaged around in the shed and came up with mumma's gold Christmas paint and he poured it into pa's spray gun and sprayed the whole cage gold like a gift from heaven. The strange naked little creature huddled in the corner and hissed at him but it wusnt no good. When I came down later to feed it, I saw that the paint had laid stripes of gold across its flesh that shimmered in the dark of the basement and gave me the horrors. I told him, I said, well Harley Miller, now look what youve gone and done, youve turned it into a tiger. Or sumthing, I said. And Harley asked slowly, looking at me the whole while with eyes as big as mumma's teacups, *Tasmanian* Tiger you mean? And then he planted a wet smackeroo across my lips just like the old days and said, Cherysh Joy Miller, you must be some kind of born genius, and then he got me to paint a sign for the cage on account I was the one good with letters. And then, Harley and me and our very own Tasmanian Tiger, with a sign in gold saying *Tru*

Taz—Found in the Wild, we wus on the road. Well we made enough to buy mummas wedding ring back from the hangman. Hed helped hisself to one of the old diamonds glued onto the band by stew and sweat and hand cream, but we was able to sell it and buy us a brand new steel cage—the creature had got so big now that Harley wusnt going to take no chances. I wus worried at first but it seemed to take to life on the road. It had been pale when we found it in the basement—pa run off and mumma in custody— hairless and sexless to boot. But now it begun to grow teeth and the painted gold stripes cut into the flesh, a living cage of golden bone frilled with seeping crimson and not just one, but two sexes, male and female. A twofer, Harley said, proud as punch.

I worry if the cage will be big enough then or strong enough, but I dont say nuthing to Harley about Taz's pointed teeth, another row growing behind the ones at the front. At feeding time, I tell Taz everything will be okay, but they gnash those needle teeth— discoloured as mummas ring—and their diamond eyes glisten at me from the corners of the cage, unblinking and hard with vengeance. Our very own Tru Taz and a twofer to boot, right where they have to be. Where we can see them, Harley says, and keep them.

For now.

JSB

The Comet

They all said in the village that the comet was a bad omen. The priest himself had looked worried during the following Sunday's preach. Although the fields had been safely reaped, the air smelling of sun and dust, and the fountain gurgling faintly in the centre square, an uneasy quietness had fallen onto the roofs and streets. The comet had spread its golden tail across the sky, straight and ominous like an angel's sword. Some said it was Gabriel coming down to punish us, while others thought it might be Michael coming to save us — there were rumours the war was near, that the king was dying, that the plague would kill us all. The Gypsy woman had spat on the ground when my neighbour had asked her at the fair what the comet meant and had refused to read his future.

It was also the night my husband died, choking under the pillow I was holding over his drunkard face. No more fists breaking my bones, no more words burning like acid, no more rapes in the silent night, his large hand covering my mouth. I had killed him while everybody was out watching the comet, taking advantage of the commotion it had created, while all the inquisitive eyes were staring at the sky. Once done, I had quietly joined the gawkers and to me, that fiery ball ploughing through the night sky looked like a lucky sign. When I got home, I screamed and cried, calling his name, and many said it was the comet that had killed him, bearer of ill times. I agreed with them, of course, drying my tears with a large handkerchief. But during the funeral, I dearly prayed to my unknown fiery guardian angel, thanking him for my freedom.

SD

Fireproof

Flames. As dire and cold and blue as blazes. The Fire Chief surveys the damage, badass pro in Nomex pants. She should be used to it by now, but the smell of seared memories in these old places gets her every time—how best to describe it? She steps over melted linoleum once oxblood red, probably, now the striated medium-rare of roadkill. The reek of burning impossible to remove from her hair for days.

Their bodies have been removed. The invalid wife, a poet, discovered dead on the day bed in the porch, the husband collapsed on the stairs—the smoke got to him before he could get to her and the flames did the rest. The Chief has a sense of being watched.

She looks up and behind the house there, plain as day, is the Fire Starter standing between two slender ghost gums—fucker, she thinks. Always one step ahead.

The Chief crunches rubber boots over glass sprinkled across the boards like an early snow, pressed-metal ceilings flapping loosely from one or two remaining rafters. The photographed grandchildren, flung by the heat from unnumbered frames, have no eyes.

The late-summer sun has just risen. Behind the

house is a yard, and behind that the smoking bush rises to the gaunt lavender hills—the Fire Starter still watching. The word nemesis comes to her mind. Ancient foe. Flash of horns and an oxblood smile.

She steps over a porcelain cat beyond saving, the real one a furry reek. The Chief will not cry. Her job is to be fireproof, good with an axe. All around her a relentless drip from the hoses now curled within the belly of the truck outside. Its lights still spinning across her reflective stripes. Neighbours gather.

"Such a dear old pair. He'd been a vet, retired. She was a poet, suffering from some underlying dementia. Not much money. Son a chef in Sydney, an adopted daughter who gave them grandchildren. They never complained."

They have stories of their own—the fire season has been hell this year. An auntie trapped inside her car. The vet up all night euthanizing koalas.

Lonely country road of life.

The Chief hears something. She'd been expecting it but her flesh crawls anyway. The ghostly murmurs are different every time, and only seen from the edge of a brimming eye.

"Can't complain, love." It's the dead husband, emerging from the ruins. "We got what we asked for. A deal's a deal."

When the Chief looks to the ravaged treeline, The space between the two ghost gums now empty. The Fire Starter may be gone, but the crackling echoes of his whisper remain.

Burn down the house.

Through the husband's immaterial trousers, the

Chief can see shattered door frames, a blackened refrigerator. His wife rises from the day bed where a moment ago she was lifeless, her skin seared in strips. Her nightgown drags in the soot. "Come on," he says. "We have to go now. A deal's a deal."

But she looks back over her shoulder at the Chief, weeping fighter of fate. "What big gloves you have," the dead poet says with a touch of envy.

The Chief can see the ghosts quite clearly against the tangerine tinge of sun-up, because they are leaving and because they are blue. And blue, she remembers, is the opposite colour to orange. Some say the world will end in fire, and so on and so forth. Huh. They are young again, these ghosts— the poet's hair as thick and flowing as ever, her eyes are glittering vertical flames in a face the dead blue of mould. Watching the old folks begin on a lovers' journey where none can follow, the Chief wonders about the exact nature of the deal the husband made with the Fire Starter to bring his wife back to him and to herself. She thinks about how the wily devil has been eluding her forever, a decade at least— will she ever catch up?

What would she do in the same position as the old couple, when given a choice between "can't complain" and "burn down the house," the later might seem like as good a choice as any?

What would anyone do?

The Fire Starter has no answer. He has gone on as always, one step ahead. Maybe two.

JSB

The Wedding Ring

The magpie held a ring in its beak, shining hard under the noon sun. I stopped in my tracks, coming back from the fields. It was hot and my vision was blurred by the sweat rolling down my forehead, but I could see the bird, perched on the fence. Slowly, slowly, I sank down and grabbed a rock, which I deftly threw at the bird. I knocked it down and almost screamed with joy, although I knew it was bad luck to kill a magpie. Its head was bloody and its beak was open. In between lay the ring. It was made of silver and had a greenish stone. A woman's ring. A lady's ring. I pocketed it, wondering where the goddamned bird had stolen it from. I felt rich, I felt happy. I was going to give it to my love and she would be happy. When I took her hand and passed the ring on her beautiful finger, she became pale and began to tremble. I asked her what troubled her so, and she said it was her mother's ring, which she had been buried with eight months ago. We went to the cemetery and found the grave undone, the body lying next to the box like a repulsive rotten old tree. I told her a bird had given me the ring, but she didn't believe me.

And neither did the policeman, nor the judge, nor, I am sure, the hangman setting the noose around my neck.

SD

A Wild Dog

On the island of Evia, in Greece, there is a small seaside town called Karystos. It is a quiet place, sometimes plagued by violent gusts of wind that make the sun umbrellas fly on the beach and the swimmers quickly run out of the water, their lips blue with cold. At night, tourists and locals mingle in the cafés and restaurants that stand shoulder to shoulder along the small harbor. Sailboats rock slowly under the summer moonlight, long tree ghosts creaking in the semi-darkness. There is a wild dog too, a long-haired mongrel of some sort, looking like a mix of a collie and a rottweiler. It trots alone along the quays and in between the tables on the terraces, never stopping for a rest. It has mad eyes too, and growls if a child or a grown-up extends a patting hand. People avoid him as much as they can, as he has bitten more than a few good-meaning victims in the past. Nobody knows where he rests or sleeps. He endlessly trots within the city, like a lost soul. A local legend says that only one person can approach him, every 15th August at midnight. A woman, all dressed in black, is supposed to appear by the Venetian tower at the west end side of the quay and call the dog by its name. Nobody can agree on the name—some say it's Stavros or Sothis, while others say it's Christodoulos or Chrysanthos. In any case, the dog comes running to her and she kneels next to him, hugging him and crying. They remain so for a long while before she stands up and walks away, leaving the animal behind, whimpering and barking helplessly. Nobody knows who the woman is, or if she still comes back. Yet, they all avoid the dog with the wild and crazy human eyes.

SD

Yellow

The last time we see the new mailman, my twin brother Peter is out watering the lawn. I'm inside at my computer, thinking how it's too late in the morning for watering, almost ten. The sun will burn the grass, for sure. I stand up and move from my office on the porch through the shadowed dining room. I hesitate at the big pine dresser that our mother moved over the basement door because it gave Peter nightmares. It is then that I hear the mailman's call:

"Y'ello!"

He's been saying it all summer—filling in for the regular guy—and at every mailbox along his route. I raise my hand to wave at him from the porch—lower it before he can see me. He must be mid-late forties—our parents' age—medium height with a small pot belly, straw coloured hair that sticks out every which way. Peter always says hello back—he sets his clock by it. The Miller place is next door, and it is half a mile before the Van de Poel's farm so by then the "y'ellos!" will be getting faint. By the time he gets to the Star-Brite Drive-In on the outskirts of town, the mailman's call will have faded into the pressing silence of a hot summer's day.

We call him Mr Yellow.

The heat hits me like a blanket. The mailman is about to get back on his rickety Schwinn with the two bags of mail hanging off the rear rack, when two men step out of a car parked across the road. When did it pull up? I only notice it when they get out of it, like they've stepped through a door out of thin air. I think, stupidly, "rerun." Or sequel maybe. I don't know why I think that. Too many movies, I guess. Our parents were crazy for movies—*films*, Dad called them—which is possibly why Peter had so many nightmares. The SUV has black windows, black hubcaps. The men wear ordinary chinos and polo shirts and their eyes are in shadow because of the long-billed caps they wear.

They cross the street and speak quietly to Mr Yellow—so quietly that the world has to hold its breath—while Peter stands on the grass staring, water from the hose making a pool of silver at his feet. And I can see the reflection of the black car in the water, and my teeth chatter in the sun as I watch the men in the reflection lead Mr Yellow over to the car and lift the Schwinn into the trunk. Then they open the back door for him to get in, slam it shut and drive away.

The next day a different guy comes by to deliver our mail. He is on an electric bicycle, which seems like a good idea, and I go outside to ask him why *our* Mr Yellow never got one of those to make his rounds easier, but the new mailman looks like he has no idea what I'm talking about.

"Who?" he says.

"The other guy," I say.

"I been doing this route for twelve years," he says. "There is no other guy."

Then he zooms away, sounding like a big mosquito. No "y'ello!" or anything. The only mail is a flier for the Star-Brite Drive-In. When I turn around, Peter is on the porch staring after the mailman, and his chin bunches up just like it did when he was six.

"Go inside, Peter," I say.

He goes into his room off the dining room which we don't use any more, and I stand in front of the big ugly dresser blocking the basement door, still crammed with the dishes that our mother collected from garage sales. *Vintage*, she called them. I call out to Peter that the first summer screening at the Star-Brite is going to be one of my favourites, *Donnie Darko*, although that is really his favourite, because of the Tears for Fears Song, "Mad World," which is really, no kidding, my favourite, and we are always like that. Fighting over whether something is his favourite or mine, who is right and who is wrong. He always says that Star-Brite is *my* favourite thing, not his—his is caramel slice—and I always say that the movie night should be his favourite, because of how he majored in Film in his freshman year before dropping out. But he says that was only because our mother made him, although in truth, it was Dad who said we should study film, as a portal, he'd said, into the soul of the world.

"A window, honey," our mom had corrected. "The expression is that the eyes are a window to the soul,

71

not a portal." And she made a frame with the thumb and forefinger of each hand.

"I feel I like the word portal better," Peter had said. I remember that. And I remember saying, "You would," or maybe I only thought it.

"What if the world doesn't have a soul?" I'd said instead, just to be a smart-arse.

My mother's face got that bunched, scared look again, the one that always made Dad take her hand, Peter and me scraping our chairs back from the dinner table and making a beeline for our rooms.

Dad dragged us to the Star-Brite every year to watch summer screenings sitting on a scratchy blanket, interrupted by faulty projectors or stoned projectionists or rain or a plague, one year, of slugs because of the rains. Our parents disappeared during our first year at university, leaving a yellow Post-It note stuck to the fridge for us to see when we came back for the summer break. No caramel slice cooling in a tin. No parents, just the yellow Post-It note with Dad's spidery back-slant. "Gone on a cruise. Spur of the moment." There was something after that, but it had been scrawled over.

I'd never seen a Post-It note in our house—our parents weren't that organized. Usually it was a phone message scribbled on a scrap of brown paper torn from a grocery bag or one of our dad's equations on the back of an envelope. Mrs Miller from next door said she saw our parents going into a black SUV parked on the side of the road—she hadn't seen it pull up, or even noticed it at first. Not until the men got out in their chinos and caps—one of them carrying a small yellow pad in his hand. When my brother asked if it was a Post-It pad, Mrs Miller said it could have been. She was too far away to tell. "Your mom and dad must have come up in the world," Mrs Miller had sniffed, "for a limo to take them to the airport."

Eventually when Peter doesn't bother to argue, to tell me that *Donnie Darko* is his favourite, not mine, and the world has to have a soul, because if it doesn't then maybe Mother and Dad never existed either, like Mr Yellow—I go back into the kitchen and throw the flier into the trash and start to shred cabbage for dinner. I smell paint. I know what Peter is going to do next. I've been through this before.

In the cool of the evening I go out to water the lawn. My brother still hasn't come out of his room, although it's time to set the table. I'm standing behind Mum's rose bush which could have, I recall, partly hidden the arrival of the black car that took both our parents and the mailman away. I've overwatered the lawn, almost flooding it—mainly to get away from the paint fumes wafting out from under Peter's bedroom door, and also because there was nothing my mother hated more than a sad brown summer lawn. I woke in the night once, saw her standing in the front yard in her nightgown, with the hem stuck to her legs, the running hose forgotten in her hand and her head lifted to the sky.

"Look," she'd said, when I joined her shivering on the threshold. "Saturn! That pale yellow guy up there? Roman God of plenty. And peace."

"He ate his own children," I said.

Her face bunched up. "But that's another story."

A petal from the yellow rose bush drifted to the wet grass at her feet.

The last time Peter painted his room was that day of the yellow Post-It note, after our parents disappeared. I waited a good six weeks before I dared to go in and wallpaper over the yellow paint. He didn't speak to me for a month claiming that I'd shut the portal to wherever they'd come from and now we'd never get back.

The yellow Post-It note was a clue, he'd said. And the yellow rosebush too. Hadn't I ever noticed that the house itself had once been painted yellow? He showed me where you could still see it where the white had peeled off.

And the first Mr Yellow was another clue. Our guy. How could I have missed it? After they disappeared, Peter explained (as if he needed to), someone had sent Mr Yellow across from our home world, somewhere near Saturn, to protect us.

"Someone?" I'd said. "You mean like an alien."

He nodded, crying. "Like us," he'd said. With Mr Yellow gone, he'd said, there was no one to protect us until we could go to our home-world again.

"Home," I said. "You mean, Saturn?"

"Wherever," he'd shrugged. But the men in black would come back and the next time it would be for us.

"The new mailman," I'd said. "He works for them?"

"We have to get out," Peter warned. "We have to

get back to Yellow. Where we belong."

Peter's room will be yellow again soon. And then he'll start on the rest of the house. And this time I won't stop him. Once when I was little and Peter was too young to remember, except in his nightmares, we'd snuck down to see the ship below ground in the basement behind the sideboard blocking the door—call it a portal. Between us, we'll figure out how to get it started again. We have to.

The setting sun turns the lawn into a lake of fire.

JSB

A Bunch Of Roses

A young lad from a good family had decided to throw a party in the large hall of his mansion. There were many guests and many distractions organized. People from the village were asked to send their best products and some were even invited to sell their goods—a knife-maker, a belt-maker, a flower-seller. She was a beautiful girl, who sold the most fragrant and delicate roses at the market. Some said her flowers came from magic, as she had been a Gypsy baby abandoned by her mother and raised by the local witch—at least, that was what many thought the old woman living on the outskirts of the village was. The young lad had secretly taken a fancy to her and had organized the feast so he could trap her inside his walls. Late in the night, drunk and fiery, he grabbed her by the waist and tried to steal a kiss from her. She slapped him and struggled to free herself. Mad with rage, he threw her roses in the chimney fire and tried to kiss her again. With a violent push, the girl managed to free herself, but fell backwards and cracked her skull against the fireplace's mantle. As he knelt next to her in a panic, she whispered these words:

"Roses will the death of you."

The young man was soon released from prison because all agreed it had been an accident (and many were well paid for their advice.) Slowly, as time passed, the young lad forgot about the incident and decided to travel.

One night, in an inn, he saw that the owner, a majestic lady with a sensuous mouth, was smiling at him. He bought some more wine and they chatted well into the night. Wine helping, they ended up in his bed, where he passed out, having enjoyed too much of the beverage. He woke up as he felt something burning slide across his throat. A splash of a red liquid that wasn't wine covered his face and as life slowly seeped out of him on the pillow in a crimson wave, he saw a man standing next to the naked woman. The stranger opened the traveller's leather pouch and exclaimed, feeling the gold: "Well, Goddamn, Rose, you fished us a good one, this time!"

SD

The Mountain

In August 1956, in the Djebel mountains during the Algeria war, a French patrol got caught in an ambush by the local fellagha, the local freedom fighters. Shots were exchanged and the patrol followed their attackers in hot pursuit. They finally came to a rocky passage and met an old man and his mule who were coming down from the opposite direction. The soldiers stopped the man and asked him if he had seen their attackers. The old man said that no, he hadn't, and that they should not go through this passage, as it was inhabited by the djinns, the spirits of the mountain, who highly disliked humans. The officer thought he was lying and to protect the fellaghas, so they tied him up and tortured him. In spite of the kicks and blows, the bloodied man still claimed he hadn't seen the guerrillas. Finally realizing that the questioning was leading them nowhere, the officer told his soldiers to shoot the man and his mule, before hiking up the passage.

Nobody heard of the patrol for days, and the commander at the camp thought they must have been killed or made prisoner by the fellaghas, but one morning, about a week later, an old man showed up at the camp

79

with the soldiers from the lost patrol tied up in a line behind his mule. Some of the soldiers were singing at the top of their lungs, others screamed continuously while a few laughed without ever stopping. They all had obviously completely lost their mind. The old man explained to the guards that he had to tie them up because they didn't want to follow him. When the commander arrived to thank the old man, he had already gone. The patrol officer was missing too, and none of the soldiers were in any state to explain what had happened to them.

The army issued a statement to the press saying the patrol had gotten lost in the mountains and had suffered from extreme sun stroke. But others said, in a lower voice and in Arabic, that they had met the djinns.

SD

The House In The Window

It is said that in Aarhus, in Denmark, there was a house with a strange story. On the first floor, in the bedroom at the left of the staircase, there was window which you couldn't open. At some point, the house was on sale, and a young couple were very interested, as it was cheap and seemed in relatively good condition. It even had its own garden, which, in the city, was a rare thing and perfect for their cat and future children. The owner, an old man, totted along as the couple visited the place. When they arrived in the bedroom, which was small but comfortable, the young woman noticed that the window couldn't open. It was summer, and quite hot. She asked the old man, who explained why, saying he hoped it wouldn't change their mind about buying the house. They laughed and said, no, of course it wouldn't. The old man told them that when you opened the window on certain evenings, a ghost house appeared in the reflection—a house that didn't exist in their street. His wife, being superstitious, had asked him to bar the window and he had left it like that, even after she died. He also added that his wife had believed that every time the house appeared, something bad would happen. The couple thought that it was a great story, and bought the house, glad to have a story attached to it. They had the window replaced with the original one before they moved in.

One evening, a few months after they had settled, the man opened the window to let some fresh air in. He suddenly noticed the reflection of an odd-looking mansion, with one window lit. He called his wife and they both marvelled at the sight and were glad the story was true. Unfortunately, the following day, their cat was killed by a speeding cat right in front of their house. They cried a lot, but life went on until another evening the woman saw the strange house's reflection in the window again, this time with two windows lit. She called her husband, and they wondered if anything bad would happen this time. During the week their car was stolen and the police found it burnt out in a field. The couple began to think the story of the house's apparition might be really true and tried not to open the window again. Time passed, and on another real hot summer night, the man got up from his bed and decided to open the window again. The ominous reflection slid on the windowpane, three windows glowing sinister. He promptly shut the window again, and didn't tell his wife, who was asleep. About three weeks later, the love of his life was diagnosed with a terribly developed cancer and died shortly afterwards.

The grieving husband sold the house to a real-estate company, who tore it down to build a new building. Nobody heard of the ghost house anymore, and no one knows what happened to the widower, except that one evening, quite drunk, he told his story to a man in a bar, who in his turn told the story to a friend of mine.

SD

On The Beach

I had been told the beach was beautiful, and it was true. I was also told that because it lay at a distance from the town, it was less crowded — and it was true too. There was a light breeze and the sea was a dark blue, bordered by the ever-changing white foam. I knew that it was considered a dangerous beach by some, with treacherous undercurrents and a swiftly changing wind. I could see that the flag by the lifeguard's chair was green and I undressed swiftly, longing for a relaxing swim.

As I rubbed sunscreen over my body, my thoughts drifted to my divorce, which was the reason I had chosen this place for a well-deserved holiday. My ex had discovered my affair with my yoga trainer — a real-life comedy situation, hadn't Paul been a powerful lawyer and I, an aspiring actress known for a full-frontal nude scene in a cable series episode. The whole thing had blown up on the social media and sleazy celebrities TV shows and I felt I needed a break from all that bad craziness. And maybe find some comfort in some beautiful boy's muscular arms. Like this lifeguard, for instance, who just lazily walked by my towel and little pile of clothes.

Incredible pale blue eyes, looking almost silver in the sunburned face. And the muscled back and thighs, oh God. Exactly what I would need.

I follow him discreetly, noticing the glances of the other female competitors as he walks by. He smells of salt, wind and another fragrance I cannot put my finger on—seaweed? Not a horrible smell, but pungent, haunting, while mild and discreet. Must be from all the swimming he must perform during the day.

He climbs on his chair and I approach him, looking up as to a heathen idol of beauty.

"Is it safe to swim today?" I ask him, wanting to hear how his voice sounds.

"Yes. You can see the flag is green," he answers, with a slight musical accent.

"Thank you. I heard this beach can be dangerous sometimes," I say, trying to sound as vulnerable as possible.

"Only for beautiful girls like you," he jokes with a wink.

I smile and turn around, slowly walking on the hot sand towards the rolling waves. I notice other women are approaching him too, a whole harem standing in front of his bare feet. He must never feel the loneliness of an empty bed, this young man!

I gasp as my feet feel the water—no matter how warm the ocean can be, the first contact with the skin is always a shock. I stand there for short while, sand running between my toes. I wonder if the lifeguard is watching me. I discreetly turn half around. He is. I resume my expedition towards the waves, knees, thighs, crotch, stomach, shoulders. The water laps my blonde hair now and I begin to swim. Oh, I love, love, love to swim. I was in the swimming team of my high-school and won many trophies. And I had beautiful, well-built boyfriends, all swimmers too. I feel the waves carry my body up and down, up and down, as my arms and legs move in coordinate action. Maybe I should pretend to drown to attract this lovely lifeguard.

The moment this thought crosses my mind, I feel my right thigh suddenly turn to wood in a painful clasp. A cramp, my panicked mind tells me. A cramp! I try to turn around, but my leg is blocked, and I begin to sink. This can't be happening, I tell myself. This can't be happening! I begin to panic and swallow a spoonful of saltwater, which makes me cough and heave.

"Help!" I cry, flailing my arms like in a bad 1950s Hollywood movie. "Help!"

I try to swim back, but my legs are dragging me down. I can't see anything anymore, only the water I splash around me, into my eyes too, burning, burning.

"Help!" I gargle.

My strength is leaving me as my head bobs up and down, over and under the water. I am about to give up all hope, when a muscular arm grabs me around the neck. The lifeguard! He has seen me and come to my rescue.

"Relax," he says. "Relax. You're with me now. You are safe."

He suddenly pushes my head under the water,

and I punch him in surprise.

"Relax," he says again, blocking my panicked blows. "You have been chosen. You are mine now. No need to panic. You will be fine. Forever."

My head goes under his powerful hand, under the surface of the sea, under the uncaring waves. Everything turns to black bitterness and salt.

Every night, I raise from the sea and walk on the beach, with the hundreds of others the lifeguard had chosen. We walk side by side, shiny and silver, unwillingly part of a destiny we do not understand. And yet, no one ever rebels. No one ever protests. Do we have a choice? What can we do against the king of the sea? What can we do against his lustful folly, immaterial puppets of a fate larger than us all? Nothing. Nothing at all. So we keep on walking and walking on the deserted beach at night, reminiscing how beautiful it looked once through our living eyes.

SD

Devil's Luck

FALL

Wranglers In Love

Topside after a staycation at the Wrangler Hotel, Ginny called Dan from a street of bland buildings pocked and stained like future ruins.

"I'd forgotten how wrong it was up here, Dan. What gives?"

It wasn't just the absence of light—it was lonelier than she remembered. Everyone looked like they were in a bad dream. Dan gave her the address of a bar. The dive, when she found it, was accessed by a long staircase through the city morgue, and it was weird tiptoeing past all those stiffs to get a stiff drink.

She found him at a booth in the back. There was a bunch of wilted daisies on the seat beside him, so she slid in opposite. Seeing him reminded her of what they were to each other and what they weren't. She put her battered Stetson on the table between them. He always liked the way that loosened her hair. She began by telling him about the Wrangler Hotel.

He shook his head, wide at the temples. The stubble on his cheeks had silvered some since the last time—how long had it been? At the Wrangler Hotel it was always daytime, she began to say, and this was always a surprise. He slammed his beer down on the table.

"Never mind all that, Gin." He leaned closer. "Go deeper?"

"Think *Gone with the Wind* meets *Unforgiven*."

He half-closed his eyes and the air around him took on a shimmer and she smelled daisies. "Take your time. I want to picture it."

A barman walked around collecting glasses and saying, "Last call."

Dan said he would kill for another. Ginny knew he was trying to make a joke because it was the price a wrangler demon named when the stakes were highest. *You'd kill for another? Another what? Oh thaaat: another minute, an extra year, or five. Are you sure, sir? Madame? And you've read the fine print? It'll cost you—you'll have to kill for it, maybe even yourself. Sign here, please.*

Ginny didn't like the way the morgue bar smelled. Like flowers and formaldehyde. It made her hungry for meat. Craven was who she was, just like anything with further to fall. She'd made her own bargains, wrangled her own second chances. You only get one and Dan was it. She should have read the fine print.

"I'm done up here, Dan. It's too hard to make a living among the living because it's not hard enough. Like shooting fish in a barrel."

"That never bothered you before." He searched her face with his daisy-yellow eyes. "You seem different somehow."

"You don't." She imagined his long fingers inching

toward the dead bouquet beside him. "Time to hang up our hats, Dan. You always said…"

"You'd do this for me?"

They left the morgue together, spurs jangling. It took them a while but down they went, down rusted manholes in cobbled streets, down unnumbered steps cut into bleeding stone, down elevators beneath potter's fields, down switchbacks beneath prehistoric lakes—until they finally got to the Wrangler Hotel. Fallen angels looking for time, they sat at the bar and drank the minutes away. The hotel was a rambling structure of stone and wood with a wide front lawn that crumbled away into an abyss. It looked like something out of a western to them, but it might look like something else to a Form Wrangler, and something else again to a Wealth Wrangler—Trump Tower meets Buckingham Palace kind of thing. Or to a Love Wrangler, the Taj Mahal, maybe. Separately, their backs to each other to hide the tears, Ginny and Dan gave words to the bargains they were finally willing to make, because if they couldn't live with each other, then they couldn't live with themselves. And in the end, the nothing of that difference was all they had left to believe in.

Bones clattered on the floor of the Wrangler Hotel. Ginny shambled through the empty tables to a large bay window, beyond which the wide sloping lawn baked under the noon day sun. The damned came out of the abyss, single file up a stony path, seeking recompense for the souls they'd sold too cheap. They milled on the front lawn, waiting for an announcement from the loudspeaker above the hotel door. Sick of waiting, a middle-aged man and a teenage girl rushed the door, stripped howling of their flesh as soon as they crossed the threshold, their smoking skeletons scattered along with the others. People got on their phones and started dialling. Mothers and lovers and children and fathers if they had them. To tell them they loved them too much, or not enough. And how they finally came to believe in the sameness of that difference.

"Last call," Ginny whispered.

"I'd kill for another." Dan's laugh was a barely audible rasp.

The whole place smelled of rotten fruit. The Announcement that finally came from the old-time megaphone was all, "Hey baby." The gathering had swelled, more of the lost waiting in the hot noonday sun, and yet there was a worrying wind gusting up that rattled the sagebrush at its edge.

"Ready steady rock," the Announcer said.

The faces of the people drained of hope because that was who they were now. A woman seeking shade under a tree started to shake and people fell to the ground and the woman's eyes ran with tears of glass that shattered her face as they fell. The ashy wind blew up from below and swirled down on the people and turned them to ash, too. Clouds massed and became a single vast dark thunderhead of regret that blotted out the sun. Dan crashed off the bar stool and started jerking like he had been tasered. Ginny shoved tables aside to get to him. The scattered bones glowed electric blue. The hot air became charged with an immense weight that pressed

Ginny to the floor. When the shocks subsided, Dan wiped at the blood on his shirt. Ginny was face-down in front of him, her tongue lolling in the dirt. Outside the thunder gradually became distant and the white light of noon returned.

"It's sucked them all back down into the chasm," Dan rasped. "They have everything they need down there."

Ginny knew they'd be back, because that's who they were. The desperados among them rushing into the bar to wrangle for their souls back, only to be reduced to scattered bones. But you get to the point where you know it's too late and there's no turning back. A door closes between you and the world. You on one side, where the clocks have stopped at midday, and not-you on the other, where the darkest hour is just before dawn.

And the difference is everything.

She noticed how Dan still clutched the daisies, wilted and missing half their petals. She pulled her tongue back into her mouth. Swallowed the toxic dust and sat up. It left a bad taste—all that soul wrangling. No price too high, no moment too small. *If I could have my time over again, I promise... just let me see her again so I can forgive...I'll wear sunscreen next time...take me back...skip that bit...fast forward, slow it down, make it last, it went so fast:* Adagio, Largo, Grave.

They paid with their souls. What else? Ginny and Dan took a percentage and the rest went to upkeep on the Wrangler Hotel.

"It wasn't the gig we asked for," Dan said. "But

it was the one we got."

"Who are the flowers for?"

He plucked a petal off his chest, its edges burnt to a crisp. "No one you know." Then he grinned through the spasms that still rippled through him and left his skin thick and silvery as a Mexican mask. Her own hair had turned blue as blazes.

"I can't believe I want you back." She elbowed toward him, combat style.

"We're necessary to the world, Gin." He held out a trembling hand. "That makes us necessary to each other."

They lay together among the bones. The ash caked to their skin. He ran clawed fingers through her hair. His touch as tender as it would always be. High noon forever.

JSB

The Fairy Wood

When the council decided to build a luxury leisure centre by the lake, many old people shook their heads and said it was a bad idea. They said it was the Fairy Wood, and that bad things would happen if people messed with it. They were, of course, laughed at. The city was desperate for money, and this project, co-financed by a famous hotel chain, sounded like a miracle.

Trouble began as soon as the project started. A bus transporting eleven workers had a mind-boggling freak accident. It occurred at night, on a straight road without any trees, but it looked like it had been rammed on the side by a speeding train, although the old tracks had been removed in 1957. There were no survivors.

A few weeks later, two other workers were found dead in a meadow. They lay on the trampled grass, one having lost his shoes and the other his jacket. They were holding each other's hand, as if they had been part of a crazy round dance and all the blood of their bodies had sprayed around them in a perfect circle.

Finally, a supervisor undressed in front of his

colleagues during a tour of the construction site and ran into the lake, where he drowned. His last words were "They are so beautiful, they are so beautiful! I want to swim with them!".

The council and the hotel company went on with the plan anyway, although there were many discussions in the council, and even a protest march trying to block the project. There was a shuffle with some police officers and it made the local TV news.

But it didn't stop the woods from being felled, the ground from being ripped open, the grass from being turned into a muddy field in which the heavy construction engines left deep tire marks.

The last element of the original landscape that resisted was a gigantic tree. It seemed unapproachable. The first wood felling team they sent was struck by lightning as a sudden storm erupted. Leaving the four men with severe burns. The second team was almost crushed by an enormous branch suddenly breaking from the trunk. The third team refused to go.

The company finally sent a bulldozer, which caught fire due to a technical problem. The second one fell into a sinkhole, killing its driver. The company decided to send three bulldozers at the same time and the tree finally fell, in a sound that some say sounded like a terrifying death rattle.

Its wood was sent to an industrial wood-mill and it is said that all those who have bought furniture made from that tree met a string of bad luck.

SD

Saint Hubertus

The legend says that Hubertus was a great hunter who one day, instead of going to church, went into the deep woods to enjoy his passion. He got lost and was wondering what to do as night was falling when a huge stag suddenly appeared in front of him. It had the largest antlers he had ever seen, its body bathed in a strange blueish light. The legend also claims that a terrifying voice told him to kneel down and worship the true god. But if many say that Hubertus recognized Christ that day, they are wrong: the hunter bowed to the only true god he acknowledged, the god of the forest, the horned god, the great and fearsome god Pan.

SD

Chronicles From Hell

*B*esides *her the beloved lies, flayed and gurgling. His skin tangled in her discarded clothes. A gelid hunk flaps across a bottle of gin. Shredded across the room like wet paperbark in a Southerly, the beloved's flesh is luscious, dusky and moist. His body? She left him an eye, and it peers out from one socket and what's left of his mouth opens in a nightmarish smile and his limbs yet twitch with life.*

You ask me what it's like, so I tell you. You ask to hear about it from the monster's mouth, so to speak. The story of Little Red from the wolf's point of view. What is it like to eat a little girl all up, wearing Granny's knickers while doing it? You scribble the question "choice?" in the margins, and in that word alone, dear author, is the hook.

The taste of him on her tongue is all that remains. She is in a frozen room somewhere in Jordaan with the cartilage of a musician's ear caught between her teeth. She must cough it up so as not to choke on it.

You write, "Lost connection between hands and heart." The nib scratches at the midnight hour, the clatter of a Hansom on the street below. Poor impulse control is the oldest meat hook in the book. Look at

103

you for example—caught between two beings, the scientist confident that consciousness is the only unquestionable fact of existence and the shaman compelled to name the unnameable. If we can know the geography of hell, you imagine, we can know everything.

She gets up to leave the beloved alone to wake, if he does, with no memory of her, alone with nothing but himself and his hunger. His body will gather itself— it has no choice—piece by agonizing piece, into some semblance of what he was, but only on the outside. On the inside he will be just like her now, for she is his maker and his mother and he is her lover and her brother. Always hungry, always alone.

It's a lot, I know, even for a philosopher such as yourself. You see yourself as a foreigner wherever you go. You recoil at the touch of my fingers on yours. I find you charming, how you still think you know where you end and I begin. You dip your pen in fresh black ink. In the margins, you scribble the word, "anthropophagy." You think words will save you. You think scientific study will keep you safe.

She is cursed. Her curse consumes her, but she can't consume it back. No. She has tried once or twice to eat herself. It doesn't stay down is the problem. Or up. Her asshole chaffed from trying to pass chunks of her own flesh. Yet she must eat and eat. And so she moves through the canal district, the boarding houses near Centraal, the brothels and then to the Noord, where she seduces a dockworker and her hunger breeds another. And if her victims survive her ravaging to flee and hunt— for themselves—the first thing to disappear is the line between dream and nightmare, between man and meat. Between you and not you.

You think anthropophagy sounds better than cannibalism. "Saturn's children," you write. "They can't help themselves."

Sometimes she thinks of the one who made her. Sometimes she thinks of me.

"The first cause?" you write. Does it matter? Was your research the cause of your corrosive desires, or vice versa? Did you cause me, or I you? Ink stains your fingers. Your eyes are ringed in red. Would we *all* not return to the father if we could, you ask. Who could blame us from trying to pry ourselves from between his ravening jaws, and force him to spit us out like so many stars? Maybe better that he chokes on us, I say. What would anyone do, at the threshold between an unliveable life and the chance to preclude one's very existence?

At the threshold of possibility, what is choice if not a subtle form of disease?

She is their maker as I was hers, bringing her to life on the page. She will be their friend. Their lover. Their sister. She will never see them again. She scribbles her tale in a cheap notebook, the stub of a candle on her nightstand more smoke than flame. Creature of lore, of legend. Of nightmare. I lock her notebooks away, for posterity, I tell her. A curiosity.

"Man eater," you write.

"Women too," she writes back.

You will be famous. They will believe as you do, the grisly memoirs you've collected, plodding from Amsterdam to Paris to London, following the

scribblings she's left behind…following them all the way to me. A black flower of ink blooms on the page. You reach for my hand, as I knew you would. Make me, you say, already slavering. Show me, you say, what it is like *there*. Where you are
   not.

JSB

Shitty Vampire

I hate the sight of blood, always have, which makes me a pretty shitty vampire and always will, not that I don't like everything else about it—taste, smell and texture—just not the slick red senseless flowering of it, and doesn't Dash have a go at me the other night after I drain a hobo dry—Dash slamming a fist into a sideview mirror for a sharp edge to cut a neat gash in his hand, and doesn't he go and smear the mess over his chin and mouth laughing and pointing at me, "Redbeard, Redbeard, haha!" and maybe it's the broken mirror, but I can't look, can I, or won't—same difference—but reach instead across to him, my Dash, and faster than light, pull his heart right out of his chest, like that—Dash's staring down at the cavity and back up at me, lips pulled back from fangs yellow in the streetlamp—there we are snapping and hissing at each other, the dead tramp our only witness. Kudzu tugging at our worn-down soles, don't we splash about in the cigarette butts and sad puddles with my Dash still holding still out a piece of smashed mirror reflecting nothing, and me holding his heart out at arm's length and breathing in the metallic living smell of it and feeling it throb and flutter in my hand like a little bird, a bird in the hand, and my Dash, my heart, is all, "Give it back, give it back, ya bastard, no joke. What if the hole closes over, then what?" and I'm like, "Then what?" So then what is that he is tossing the mirror away—fear spilling like ink from his eyes—the hole in his chest closing over, the fluttering beats in my hand slowing, slowing, slowing—do I slip it back just in time, his ribcage grazing my knuckles as I let it go? Do I set it free—and is Dash all grinning again like normal and calling me a twat and then with one hand over his heart, does he step up so close that I can smell death when he reaches across with a rag and wipes the stolen blood off my chin tenderly and quickly and stuffs the rag back in his pocket so I won't have to see it—the crimson flower of life, mine for the taking and never more to give?

JSB

Nine Silver Nails

My love has beautiful eyes
With which she can see my soul
My love has a lovely mouth
With which she can kiss my breath
My love has a lovely nose
With which she can smell my tears
My love has two small ears
With which she can hear my joy
My love has a lovely nest
In which my bird loves to hide
My love has a secret cave
In which I want to bury a treasure
And I have nine long silver nails
One for each lovely hole of her body

SD

The Gift

The students gathered in the town square. Some steepled their swollen fingers beneath their chins. Others rocked in their scuffed boots or craned their unwashed necks in order to get a glimpse of the great Wizard Hian Mitee. The crowds swelled and the wizard was glad he brought his dagger, concealed in the folds of his gown, because you never knew with these Podunk gatherings, where security was always lax, to say the least.

"Tell us what we need to know, Wizard," called a broken male voice.

"Tell us everything," called another.

"What is the secret?"

Mitee smiled his practiced smile, and then he patted the old grimoire that rested on the podium in a rehearsed gesture that was second nature by now. He laboriously cleared his throat making a pantomime out of it as he always did, to break the ice. A titter passed through the audience—they'd expected a good show. One man even guffawed. A good sign. The wizard liked a good manly guffaw, hard to come by these days, world domination not being what it was. Not many women in the crowd either, he noticed, less than usual. He decided to ask the organizers about that.

He stepped out from the podium. He walked to the edge of the stage and his threadbare robes caught on a gentle breeze that brought a whiff of saw dust and cow manure. He paused, admiring how the peaked shadow of his wizard's hat fell over their expectant faces.

"Show, don't tell," he began.

Someone gasped. A round of applause.

"Follow the sun," the wizard said, "for tomorrow the rain may come!"

"A drowning man.... or woman, " he said, lowering his voice to a whisper and raising both hands to the sky, "will clutch at straws!" The last lost in thunderous applause.

"A journey of a thousand miles," he continued when a restive sob-punctuated silence resumed, "begins with a single step."

The small crowd erupted in scattered tumult.

Self-styled scholars, their necks were sunburned from driving oxen. Their chilblained fingers stained from dispensing tonics or cutting bolts of cloth. Scholars, Hian Mitee inwardly scoffed at the crowd of would-be scholars who secretly expended their ejaculate over dreams of mythical universities in glittering cities while nodding over last year's medical journals at the municipal archives.

They waved their greasy hats in the air as one. Now they wept. Some hugged. Others fell to their knees in the mud. Others frantically raised their hands in "not so much a question as to comment," and the wizard braced himself for the part of the show he disliked the most, wishing he could still afford a bodyguard. They'd talk about the show for months until the next act rolled into town, a ragged circus perhaps, or an inebriated dramatist. Eventually they dispersed and the wizard tucked his grimoire under his arm and searched the square for his buggy, his beady eyes falling on a village boy sitting on a bench at the edge of the muddy square, peeling an egg.

The wizard gathered his robes so that they wouldn't drag in the mud and wandered over to the boy. He sat down beside him and watched in amazement as he peeled the egg. It seemed to Hian Mitee as though he'd never seen peel fall off an egg so easily. The youth's delicate thumbs delivered the shell fragments smoothly from the curved white dome of the egg, leaving it as smooth and unpocked as the wizard's own bald pate beneath his conical hat. The sun was hot and Mitee felt the sweat trickle out from under the silk rim and down his neck beneath what was left of his luxuriant white hair. Once such a hit with the female students.

Seemingly oblivious to the wizard, the young man had finished peeling his egg and bit into it and now it was the wizards turn to gasp. The yolk was a perfect yellow, not a trace of green. Like velvet, the wizard imagined, on the tongue.

"That looks like a perfectly boiled egg," Mitee stammered, trying to keep the tremor from his voice.

The village boy looked up at the wizard and

blanched as if only now realizing where he was. The wizard had once been very fond of young men like him—dreamy and awkward, brilliant but hopelessly ignorant—just the sort of acolyte you want in your corner. Now they mostly bored him.

The yokel blushed through a mouth full of egg, the tender whites and creamy yellow sticking to his slightly buck teeth. He swallowed and grinned. "Thank you, your grace," he stammered. "It's not as hard as it looks. Would you like me to tell you the secret?"

The wizard nodded so hard that his hat slipped down on his sweaty forehead, exposing his bald scalp. The student looked up at in alarm.

"Yes," the wizard rasped, adjusting the peeked hat. "Yes! The secret…"

"Not much to it, your majesty," the youth hesitated and blushed. "First you bring an inch of water to the boil…"

When he finished giving the wizard his secret to the perfect boiled egg, the wizard raised himself to his full height, drew his dagger and slit the boy's downy throat from ear to ear. As soon as he was sure the young man was perfectly dead, he extended a pointy finger and made the corpse disappear in a puff of yellow smoke, blood and all. After he was gone, he smooshed all traces of the egg into the dirt with the heel of his goatskin slipper, so that no sign of the tender whites, or silky yolk remained.

His memory not being what it was, he quickly scribbled the instructions for boiling the perfect egg in invisible ink in his grimoire. Then he replaced the dagger in its scabbard, adjusted his conical hat onto his head and went back to his high tower in a land far away. One evening, soon after he returned, his acolyte—once a dreamy unambitious youth now well into stiff middle age—set a tray of buttered toast, tea, brandy, and two boiled eggs before the wizard. "I don't know how you do it, master," he said, discretely closing the wizard's grimoire to make way for the tray. "Keeping all those adoring followers happy. No wonder you're exhausted."

They had both tacitly and wordlessly agreed never to discuss the blood caked on the wizard's slippers, and the acolyte had somehow known, because he lived not for himself but for the one he served, to dispose of them in the incinerator, and to commission new ones which had arrived earlier that morning. All very much to the wizard's satisfaction. The village boy's slim fingers clawing at the crimson gurgling grin across his innocent throat flashed momentarily before him, before he blinked it all away and sat back in his chair. He took one of the peeled eggs in his pointed fingers, held it aloft like a crystal ball.

"The secret to success, my dear fellow, is to give them what they want," he said, "and never what they actually need."

Despite following the village boy's recipe faithfully, the eggs peeled with difficulty and were rubbery on the tongue, the yolks dry and tasteless. But the wizard choked them down, every chalky crumb, before sitting back with his brandy and his feet in their new slippers resting on a footstool, and the happy thought that one day very soon, with his knowledge of how to boil the perfect egg, he would rule the world.

JSB—for Seb Doubinsky

The Widower

I always enjoy reading in cemeteries, and when I lived in Paris, my favourite place was the Père Lachaise. Built on a large hill, it is a true necropolis, a city of the dead, with its mausoleums standing along the paved alleyways like small houses in a city.

That day I had found the perfect spot, a bench under a yellowing tree. I opened my book and was well engaged with it when suddenly I heard some yelling behind me. I was shocked, as silence is as sacred in a cemetery as it is in a library. I turned around and saw, in the distance, in the middle of an uneven row of tombs, a man circling around a grave, cursing and flailing his arms in the air. He was all dressed in black and his hair was snow white. A bunch of red roses lay at his feet.

Casting my irritation aside, I pricked my ears to understand what he was saying. "OH, how could you do this to me!" he cried. "How could you do this to me!" His voice was loud and clear in the autumn silence and I was wondering when one of the keepers would show up and tell him to calm down. He sounded furious, exasperated, full of rage. I was waiting for him to kick the gravestone or do something else drastic. The man is mad with grief, I thought. How much one must be in love to act this way. His wife must have passed away recently, and he just can't bear it.

Suddenly, as to confirm my thoughts, the man sank to his knees and began to sob, his forehead resting against the cold marble. Deciding I should leave this poor man in peace, I concentrated on my book again and my thoughts slowly floated away from the striking scene I had just witnessed. I heard him sob for a while, then nothing. Raising my eyes from my book, I noticed he was gone.

Later, as the sky turned a darker blue and the wind blew with an evening chill, I decided it was time go home. The row of tombs being on my way to the exit, I decided to stop by the grave, which was easy to spot because of the brand-new rose bouquet that stuck out like tiny blood pearls. Raising the collar of my coat, my feet digging deep in the gravel, I made my way to the stage of the scene I had witnessed. If the wind was indeed chilly, it was a damp coldness of another kind that suddenly grabbed me as I deciphered the sparse inscribing on the headstone:

Amélie Collin, 1812-1873.

SD

The Herbarium

This house has a story, you know. Or rather, the garden of this house has one. Yes, it is beautiful. Quite unusual with its four statues at the corners and its lovely stone bird bath in the middle. But some say it changes at night and becomes, how should I put it, different. Oh, I never experienced it, but my grandmother said the woman she bought the house from did. It is actually quite the story, I must say.

Apparently, it all began when the former owner — I shan't reveal her name, for obvious reasons, but I will call her Mrs. B**** — had a leak in the garden, at the foot of the bird bath. She called a local plumbing company to come and fix it, and they dug a big hole. To everybody's horrified surprise, the workers found a skeleton and a book, a very old, heavy book, bound in what had been some precious fabric.

Of course, the police came and all, there was an investigation, and it was found that both the body and the book were from the 16th century. Doing some extra research, the local archivist found out that the body must have been Lord T****, one of the ancestors of the family, who apparently had expressed the desire to be buried in his garden. He showed Mrs. B**** the will and the signature, most ornate as it was the fashion at this time. As she was the sole heir to the lord, the book was given back to her, a piece of family lore one would say.

The book was actually an herbarium, but of the strangest kind: the flowers and herbs in it didn't appear to resemble any known species, or at least were unknown to Mrs. B****. There were descriptions under each specimen, but unintelligible, due to Lord T****'s impossible handwriting. What was also out of the ordinary was that the flowers had no colours, or rather, only a strange hue, between silver and gray. It was probably due to the passing of time, Mrs. B**** surmised, as she put it in a glass-cased shelf in her library.

Now, Mrs. B**** had a young daughter whom I will call Anna, to make it simple. Anna was thirteen years old, and a little bit of an original soul. She managed school alright, but what she liked most was art classes and reading poetry. She took a peculiar, but not altogether surprising, interest in the strange old book, which she opened and consulted often. She even took a long time to decipher her ancestor's handwriting, which she managed to do quite well, to her mother's surprise.

"These are dream flowers, mommy," she explained one day. "It's written here, in the beginning."

"Dream flowers?" Mrs. B**** said, a little perplexed.

"Yes! Lord T**** writes here that he picks them up when he walks in the garden at night. Well, in his dreams. That's why they're so strange. And beautiful," she added with a strange light in her eyes.

Nonsense, Mrs. B**** thought, but just nodded, not wanting to hurt her only child's feelings. Anna, however, began to speak of strange things that alerted her mother. She talked about walking in the garden at night, and talking to a strange lady who was gardening there.

In the beginning, Mrs. B**** thought it was one of her child's many fancies—after all, she had had an invisible friend for many years when she was younger—but Anna seemed to be losing more and more touch with reality, waiting with impatience for night to come, as if her real life began then.

One day, Mrs. B**** walked into Anna's room to clean while she was at school and found the herbarium opened on her bed. She had allowed the child to keep it in her room, as long as she took good care of it. But what she saw sent an icy shiver down her spine: there were new flowers added on the pages of the book, with Anna's distinctive handwriting under it.

Although she felt panicked at first, she managed to keep her senses, and she went to visit the archivist to see if he could investigate more about Lord T****. He promised he would inspect the archives to see what he could find.

In the following days, Mrs. B**** listened more attentively to her daughter's descriptions of the garden at night and her worries morphed into anguish. It sounded as if Anna liked the ghostly place better than real life. To make things worse, the archivist had some news. Over tea, he told Mrs. B**** that he had found the correspondence of lady T****, the lord's wife, with her sister. Apparently, Lord T**** had gone mad over a couple of months, refusing to leave his room during the day, and raving about a mysterious lady friend he met every night in the garden. When he died, his wife had yielded to his last wish, which was to be buried at the foot of the birdbath, but she had insisted that the book should be buried with him.

Even if Mrs. B***** was not of a superstitious nature, the mental state of her daughter increasingly worried her. So much, actually, that she decided to burn the book while Anna was at school—she didn't want to go to school anymore, and her grades were more and more terrible. Having a servant light the chimney although it was a warm month of May, she threw the book amidst the flames, but, to her horror, it would not burn. It seemed that the flames went through it, leaving it intact. Finally, she had an idea, secretly thanking Lady T**** for the hint. She told her frightened servant to get a spade and to dig a deep hole in the back of the garden, where she buried the book, with a heavy stone placed over it.

She was nervous to see how Anna would react when she would discover her favourite herbarium gone, but to her surprise, the child had no reaction. She went into her room, dropped her heavy schoolbag and asked for some cake. Mrs. B**** didn't mention anything, afraid her remark would trigger some anguish and waited until evening, but still—nothing. At dinner, Anna seemed happier than she had ever been for the past six weeks, not mentioning the night garden and eating with good appetite. Perplexed, Mrs. B**** finally asked her if she didn't miss her book.

"What book?" Anna answered.

"Well, the herbarium", Mrs. B****. said.

"What herbarium?"

Understanding the curse had been lifted, Mrs. B.**** let the matter drop. Then she sold the house to my grand-mother and left the country. It was the lady's servant who told my granny the story one day, when she had said she considered planting some new flower beds in the garden. What? Oh yes, the book… Well, it must still be buried somewhere under these flower beds, I suppose.

SD

Devil's Luck

Everybody knows cards and liquor attract the devil. He showed up in our town, in Leon's saloon. We all recognized him at once—elegant, dressed in black with a fancy hat and smelling of expensive cologne. I was at the table with Roy, who, as usual, was winning the game. Roy was famous in the county, hell, maybe even in the State, for never losing a game. It had almost cost him his life a couple of times, and he had the scars to prove it. The Devil must have heard about him through one of the guys Roy had to shoot down or from somebody else who knew about him. Whatever the case, he appeared, all dressed in black and smelling fancy, with a small moustache and a pointy beard, like in the pictures. He asked Roy if he was willing to play a game with him. "We'll play blackjack and I will be the dealer. I will grant you any wish if you win," he said. Roy accepted. The Devil smiled and asked Leon for a quiet room where the two of them could play in peace. Leon prepared one of the side rooms and they disappeared. We resumed our drinking and our talking, with our ears pricked for disaster.

The night dragged on and only me and a young

125

cowboy named José were left. I was drowning my sorrow of having lost my wife to a passing snake-oil seller, and he was drinking to celebrate his wedding. In any case we were there, chatting with Leon, when suddenly the Devil rushed out of the room, hopped on his black mare and left never to return. We all turned around and looked at Roy who was collecting a pile of gold on the table, laughing. He joined us and ordered a tall bottle of whiskey to celebrate.

"What in the hell happened?" I asked. "How did you beat the Devil?"

"Very simple," he answered. "I asked him if I could formulate my wish before we began the game, which was fine by him because he thought he already owned my sorry soul. And he accepted." He stopped, chugged down a shot of whiskey and filled it again. "What was your wish, pard?" I asked again, impatient to hear the end of story. "Well, I told him I wished he couldn't cheat." I still remember Roy's laugh until this day. Later, he took his fortune and went West. And maybe the Devil did get him in the end, but then again, I don't know anything about that.

SD

Eternity (the One Who Clings)

WINTER

Endless Reflections

"This broken mirror has quite a peculiar story," my good friend—whom I shall call Pierre to respect the fellow's reputation—told me, as he noticed my perplexed look when I stepped in the warm mansion, my coat covered with a wet snowy film.

The mirror—a beautiful, heavily gilded thing hanging in the hallway of the mansion—was indeed quite an extraordinary object, as its surface was smashed in a thousand pieces, making it look like the web of an enraged silver spider queen.

"I will tell you its story later, if you're not afraid of ghosts," he said, leading me to the sitting room after I had hung my dripping coat in the hallway.

My friend handed me a whisky and we sat by the fireplace like two old men in a classic M.R. James story. It was the first time I visited my friend in his new home, a fabulous Romantic-style mansion in the heights of Montmartre in Paris. He had inherited it from his father, who had been a semi-famous underground film actor in the 50s and the 60s, then had a long career in Italy as a bad guy, monster or slasher in *giallo* movies. He had retired

131

in France and had left my friend as sole inheritor of his fortune and assets, although he had left the mother and the son in the early sixties, before moving to Italy.

"Come, I'll show you around", he said as we had emptied our glasses and chatted about trivial matters, as old friends do.

We went through rooms and hallways and a huge kitchen and up some stairs and saw more rooms and up some more stairs again and saw even more rooms, all in the same chic but gloomy style.

"Quite a place, eh?" Pierre said as we were coming down the last flight of stairs. "My old man seemed obsessed with 19th century gothic... Imagine my shock when I walked in for the first time!"

We passed the strange mirror again, and I asked him about it.

"Well, to be honest, it's a very creepy thing. I was told by an old acquaintance of my father that it was supposed to be the true inspiration for Oscar Wilde's Portrait of Dorian Gray, you know the story with the painting aging while its owner remains young. Apparently the mirror had the same power. And maybe still has," he added, somewhat sombrely.

"How do you mean?" I asked, genuinely interested. I knew my friend wasn't the superstitious kind—he was a renowned professor of philosophy, known for his extremely rational position. Out of curiosity I approached my face to the uneven and shiny surface.

My friend's swift hand on my chest interrupted me getting any closer.

"Don't do that," he said, nervously. "I can assure you, it's not a joke."

Brushing his hand aside, I took a good look at the shattered thing. At first, I saw a hundred tiny reflections of myself but something didn't seem quite right.

As I inched even closer, I heard my friend let out a powerful "No!" but it was too late and I realized my mistake. The faces in the mirror were mine alright, but much younger, when I was still a young boy. I even recognized the t-shirt with the cartoon character I was wearing, but the face...oh, the face: it was deformed by a malignant and perverse smile, and through the eyes shone a dark light that seemed intent on fascinating me.

I was suddenly pulled back by my friend and I stared at him, completely at a loss for words.

"It took me ten minutes to pull you away," he said.

By the sweat that shone on his forehead and stained his white shirt in various smelly circles of gray, I saw that he wasn't lying.

"You should get rid of it," I said, my voice trembling.

"I can't," he said. "I have tried to pull it off the wall, but it won't budge. And the worst part is that every day, when I pass in front of it, I feel like looking into it..."

We had a stiff whisky in his dining room and little by little chatted about other things. I never visited him again, nor he invited me. I haven't seen him since, although some mutual friends tell me that they run into him once in a while, and that he still looks very young for his age.

SD

Eternity

A long time ago in Poland, in a forgotten shtetl beside a faraway wood, there lived a humble book illustrator with his young wife, Anna, and the orphaned infant of her sister. The illustrator worked hard to support his little family but at heart he didn't want to be a book illustrator—he wanted to be a real artist with patrons from the decadent salons of Krakow. Nothing his pretty young wife Anna could say made him feel any better. Every winter he felt his hopes of fame and fortune recede and the dark maw of despair open before him like a cave in one of his own inconsequential illustrations.

One day, although Anna begged him not to, the artist announced he was venturing into the woods to seek help from a witch who lived within, a craven hag rumoured to serve the One Who Clings.

"I just need a spell to make me famous." The illustrator's pockets bulged with the last of their savings for the witch was rumoured to be very expensive. "I'll be home soon."

He had recently been passed over yet again by a third-rate gallery in Krakow—his wife jiggled her sister's babe—a tearless, sickly child—and went back inside their little house. There was nothing she could do to stop him.

The trees closed around the artist as he walked deeper and deeper into the forest, and into silence in which not even the birdsong penetrated. Eventually he got to the witch's hut, a half-collapsed shanty with none of the trappings of enchantment that the illustrator had so often tried to capture in his inconsequential drawings.

The door was open and he stepped in, but all was dark and although he could smell burned food, the witch herself was nowhere to be seen.

"Help me," he begged the darkness.

The witch had heard it all before—she was older than old. But perhaps because she was miffed at the artist not bringing gifts, or how his face convulsed in disgust when he finally spotted her sitting on a stool in a dank corner, at first she refused. She shook her head, dribbling bitter tea onto the pelt of a rank familiar that could have been a cat...once.

"The cost is higher than you can pay," she gibbered, poking at the coins he'd thrown on the table. "Eternity isn't cheap."

The illustrator's eyes had indeed adjusted to the darkness. Unable to bring himself to look at the witch directly, due to her backward facing knees and yolky drool, he found himself staring instead into his own reflection in the mirror behind her. There he saw the true artist, not as he was, but as he was destined to be.

"Name your price," he said.

And so it was done. The sorceress took her bone

nib, dipped it in red and wrote four words down on a gluey strip of wet parchment and instructed him how to grind vermillion for the invocation from precious cinnabar, and then how to inscribe the words onto a still wet canvas.

"I'm an artist," he grumbled. "You don't have to tell me."

"Watercolours are a law unto themselves," she warned, "the pigments can bloom in unpredictable ways."

But he was already out the door and rushing home through the pale still boughs of the forest. He went straight up to his garret and did as the crone said, concealing the four words of the curse in a charming watercolour of an ogre and a gutsy princess.

At that moment, a door cracked open to eternity, and a demon appeared on the threshold. Its skin was pasty and red worms squirmed on its scalp instead of hair. The demon slithered onto the artist's back and introduced itself. But the artist already knew.

It was the One Who Clings.

Things changed quickly after that. From far and wide, critics and dilettantes alike spoke of the artist's uncanny genius. He moved his family to Krakow to be closer to the galleries and dance halls. He furnished their villa with mirrors on every surface, all the better to see himself from every angle, the artist he was destined to be. Every day the curse cleverly concealed in his work wormed its way into the souls of all who gazed upon it. In the artist's very perfection now lay the end of all hope.

Anna—forbidden from entering her husband's

studio lest she too fall into the infernal clutch (he retained at least that much humanity)—wept for the simple life she'd left behind. She no longer knew the man she married, replaced by a distorted, corrupt version of himself, bent from the weight of the horror piggybacked to his very soul. One day, she called a rabbi to their glittering hall of mirrors, but after a half-hour with her husband, he told Anna not to send for him again. "I can do nothing for this man," he said.

Anna rode back to the shtetl determined to confront the meddling crone who stole her life. Perhaps because of the honey cake Anna remembered to pack into her basket, or because she did not recoil at the witch's backward facing knees, or perhaps knowing that Anna was with her own child—the witch readily agreed, for she served two masters. In vermillion, she scribbled the four words of the curse as before, but added a fifth word, dipping her bone nib into quicksilver, and told Anna how to conceal this word—the one that would transform the curse into a blessing—onto her husband's canvas while it was still sticky. "The moment of letting go," the witch hissed. "Don't forget."

Anna poured gold onto the table, but the sorceress would take no money—she saw that the cost would be high enough. Or perhaps her suppurated mouth was too full of the honey cake, crumbs of which snowed down on the familiar at her feet, which had been and clearly still was, a cat.

Anna went back to the city and did as she was told—oh he'd have killed her if he'd known. With trembling hands, she blended the red letters of the curse into the damp folds of a watercolour toadstool, quickly adding the silvered antidote. Instantly, a strong wind gusted in from the windows of the studio, and the babe in her arms stopped her tearless fretting and her eyes glittered like stars. Anna's blood ran cold. Bells pealed the dark hour and from her husband's bedchamber, she heard him howl.

"It is done," Anna thought, without saying its name out loud, because she'd invoked the most powerful and secret spirit of all—the spirit of Letting Go. She went running to attend to her husband, only to find a soul in tatters and a body ravaged from the inside out. By the morning he was dead.

Such is the way with these things.

The sale of the villa was barely enough to cover her husband's debts. Anna returned to the shtetl and soon after, she gave birth to a baby girl. One day, stumbling upon some canvases her husband had left behind—stacked and pale and shimmering in the last of the light—she began to paint. Penniless and alone, what choice did she have?

She was a quick study, soon overtaking her husband's dearly bought genius. Critics raved. Buyers came from as far as Warsaw, rich burghers whose attraction to the pretty widow's shtetl art could only be explained by the way it made them feel free of heart and pure of soul. The great German art philosopher Walther Winkler swore that in the wry, patient gaze of her doomed rabbis and milkmaids and matchmakers, he felt "as it were, an inimitable imitation, if that were possible, of...love."

Anna paid no attention to their praise—she had enough to think about running her house and bringing up her girls, while keeping up with the demand for her paintings. Every week, she sent her daughter with a basket of wine and honey cakes to visit the old witch deep in the forest. Alone and arthritic, the witch and her purring familiar lived for the wine and warm honey cake and the child's tales of scrambling through thicket and shallow stream, and in return she blessed the girl with not one artistic bone in her body.

Anna's clinging grey-eyed niece was not so lucky. Shadowing her aunt like a cat, the strangeling's tread was so silent that Anna insisted she wear a silver bell around her neck lest she startle her to death. The girl was a fast learner, a prodigy, proficient at blending the vermillion and silver invocation into the wet hair of a gravedigger, or the sticky gleam of the mezuzah, or the shtetl streets in all their imperfect beauty. Anna loved her girls equally—the wild child of the woods, and the watchful mute at her heel who understood, without Anna having to tell her, that true art is both a blessing and a curse, a clinging and a letting go—and that the hard-earned magic lies in finding a balance between the two.

JSB

The Godless Rabbi

In a small town near Odessa, in Ukraine, lived a Rebbe who one morning suddenly declared he didn't believe in God anymore. His wife was desperate, his children were desperate, the village was desperate. The wife cried: "How are we going to eat if you quit your job?" The children cried: "The whole village is going to make fun of us and throw stones in our direction!" The villagers cried: "Who is going to take care of the Shabbat and bless our homes?"

A man suddenly came running to the square where everybody had gathered, trying to make the Rebbe change his mind. "The Cossack are coming! The Cossack are coming!" "Do not fear and follow me quickly!" the Rebbe said, leading them all into the Synagogue.

He closed the door, locked it and told everyone to be quiet. The Cossacks arrived and began shooting their guns in the air, cracking their whips and yelling insults. They were obviously looking for the villagers, but strangely couldn't find them.

Inside the Synagogue, all trembled with fear as the Cossacks passed to and fro outside, their heavy boots stomping in the mud and snow. The soldiers remained for a couple of hours, looting what they could, but finally left, screaming obscenities as they rode away.

The Rebbe opened the doors again and let everyone out. "Rebbe, Rebbe," they cried, "How can you not believe in God when such a miracle occurred? The Cossack didn't find us, and we were right here, under their noses. You must believe in God again, Rebbe!" But the Rebbe shook his head, smiling. "If I had believed in God, dear friends, we would all be dead now."

SD

The Crying Tree

A nd you see, over there, the tree on top of the big hill? We call it the crying tree. Yes, it looks like it's crying, with its sad branches almost touching the ground, but the name doesn't come from its shape. It's a beautiful tree, I agree, but it wasn't always like that. It has brought much sadness over this land. No one can approach it without beginning to cry. I mean, you don't cry out of sadness, but your eyes begin to swell, itch and water and suddenly tears run endlessly on your cheeks. You can't help it. We have all tried, as children.

Oh yes, this region has a lot of legends, darling. That's why I wanted to bring you here: you told me you loved folklore and old women's tales. Well, here you go. The crying tree. Of course there is a story attached to it. It is said that sixteen witches were hung on its branches in 1623. Well, sixteen women accused of being witches. You know how it was. The youngest was only thirteen. We have all the archives in the library. One of them apparently cursed the village and said whoever would approach the tree would cry their eyes out.

And it's true. You do. I've tried it. Everybody has

tried it here. It's a local attraction. The government even sent some people to study it three years ago, botanists, geologists and whatnot. Even with gas masks on, they cried. They cried so much they couldn't work. Of course there must be a natural explanation, dear. Of course. But nobody has found it yet. So it's still the crying tree and the tree of the witches. It also said that the only person that won't cry near the tree is the Devil. Shall we try and see if you cry too, my darling? What? You don't feel like taking such a long walk now? It's not that far and it's worth it, I promise. It's good to cry, once in a while. To really cry. I know you claim you never do. But nobody can resist the crying tree. Not even you—unless you're the devil, of course! Don't be a coward! Walk with me to the crying tree! We'll cry together! It will be wonderful! Sorry? What if you don't cry? Well, you're the Devil then and I'll cry for both of us.

SD

Lifeline

It was a weeknight, very late, so the club was half empty. It was freezing. There were some girls dancing and their loveliness made his eyes water but he knew that about himself, how he must reek of 40-proof loneliness. The girls slowed their dancing when he walked past like they could smell it too. Someone smiled at him from the bar and she was pretty but all he saw in her grey eyes was a reflection of his own need, so he kept on walking.

Above the urinal there was a flyer for a psychic — a palm reader. Cherry Sloane, Chirologist, the flyer said, and there were some letters after her name. Her office was upstairs, above the club. She was open late, it said. Joel washed his hands and went back to the bar. He ordered a drink he didn't want. He asked the bartender about the palm reader upstairs, and she said she hadn't heard much about her, nothing bad anyway. Joel remembered that his ex had gone to a psychic, and he wondered if that had something to do with them breaking up. When Joel was little, his mother had taken him and his brother to a carnival and they'd put money in a "Chiromancy" machine and a card popped out that told his mother's fortune, and she kept the card as a memento of one of the happiest days of her life.

Joel put down his drink and followed the EXIT signs to where a piece of paper stuck on the wall said, "Cherry's Place," with a pencilled arrow pointing up the stairs. Joel felt a twinge in his chest, as if the arrow had pierced his heart. He climbed the stairs, which were wide and pocked, and the music from the club receded to a muffled thud that slowly died, like a heartbeat that stopped. He emerged in a room so dark and vast that he couldn't see the edges. Dirty windows overlooked the street below, factory smokestacks blurry behind a build-up of silt and dust on the glass. A woman sat bent over a table in the far-left corner, the glow of a desk lamp drawing all the light in the room to her face. He heard a whispering but she had her mouth closed. A slouched shadow heaved in a distant corner of the room.

He knew then that he'd made a terrible mistake. But the minute he turned to go, the woman's head snapped up and he froze. She was elderly with thinning white hair. Her face was covered in tattoos and there were tattoos on her hands, too, all the way to where her grimy cardigan covered her wrists. She had webbing between her fingers.

"Lines, ten bucks," she said. "Fifteen for mounts."

Joel wondered what kind of body-mod artist would do this to an old lady. He didn't know what a mount was. He just wanted to get out of there, but those rheumy eyes peering from their mask of ink held him in place. Most of his friends had tattoos, and he had a couple too. A hamburger on the back of one calf, and his ex's initials somewhere he'd forgotten now. The palm reader had the Milky Way tattooed across her throat, the entire solar system below that. He could see Venus from here, pulsating between the missing buttons of her cardigan.

He said, "Don't suppose you take—"

She tapped on a credit card terminal with a yellowed fingernail.

Joel sat down opposite her at the desk by the window. A streetlight infused that corner of the room with a pee-coloured glow. He could hear the rumble of trucks. He listened for music from the club below but the room was silent, except for the occasional whisper behind him that he must be imagining.

"I can't stay," he said. "Not sure how long this'll take. I'm on a dare from some friends, so…"

She'd taken his hand in her webbed ones while he was talking. Her touch gave him a jolt of nausea; spit pooled in his mouth. She turned his hand over, touched the underside of his fingers with hers. "You don't have any friends," she said.

A sound like a book dropping onto the floor made him start but she seemed not to hear it. She eyed him, still with her fingers resting lightly on his, and cradling his wrist delicately in her other hand, her pinky extended so that he could see tiny veins in the webbing.

She let go his hand—there were tissues stuffed in a teacup—still without looking at it.

"I can't take your money," she said. "Sorry."

Something in that voice said it wasn't the money she was sorry about.

"What?" he said. But he didn't stand up. "Did you see something bad? You didn't even look!" He waved his hand in front of her face. She didn't move.

He drew ten dollars from his pocket and slapped it on the table. "What did you see?"

"The light's bad," she said. "Who am I to—"

"Tell me," he said. "I can take it."

"You have no choice," she said. "None of us do." She swept her arms out across the room, exposing a swirling geography of tattoos.

"Tell me," he said.

She slumped in her seat. "The others…"

"I don't care about the others."

She pulled a used tissue from a pocket. "That changes too."

"Tell me," he said.

A tear oozed and began to fall down an impossible staircase inked on her hollow cheek.

"You will die—" she said.

Joel stood up so violently, the chair crashed onto the floor. There was a shifting in the air behind him. "Crazy bitch!" he shrieked.

He was almost at the stairs when she said, "— the moment you leave the building." Turning back was the wrong thing to do, but he did it anyway.

"What?" he said. Shapes began to solidify at the edge of his eye.

"Your life will end with you walking out of here."

He began to laugh so hard that he started to cry.

It was then that he noticed a pile of pizza boxes

on a low table. There was a mattress on the floor and a guy bent cross-legged over a book. There were others, too. All of them around his age, propped against the wall, rolling cigarettes or murmuring together like they had always been there.

A girl sat on a worn couch, trimming her brown hair with office scissors. She put the scissors on the arm of the couch and stood up.

"Welcome." Gilded hunks of blonde hair floated to the floor. "I'll show you to your room."

JSB

The Kiss

There was a house in the city that was rumoured to be haunted. The story said that a beautiful young woman, the only daughter of the household, had fallen in love with a rake, who had seduced and abandoned her. Her parents had obliged her to give her child to an orphanage, and had locked her in her room. One night, she had managed to escape, with the help of a servant who had fallen in love with her and had made a double of the key for her. She cut the throats of her parents in their sleep and hung herself on the huge chandelier that overlooked the entrance hall. The servant discovered the gruesome scene in the morning and had to be committed to an insane asylum.

A young man, who had drunk too much, told his friends he would sneak into the house and steal a kiss from the ghost who, he was sure, felt abandoned and lonely. All laughed, saying that ghosts didn't exist, and if they did, they were made of mist. The young man, vexed, left the party and was not seen anymore.

After two days, his parents asked his friends where he could be and they told the parents the story.

When the police entered the abandoned house, they found the young man still alive, but blue with cold. His lips had so much frost bite that they had begun to rot, and had to be cut from his face.

SD

The Lover

There is a life size bronze statue in a side alley in the Vienna Central Cemetery which has a peculiar tradition attached to it. It represents a man standing, his right arm slightly raised, his hand closed except for his index finger, which points at nothing in particular. He is dressed as if he was about to go out to a concert or a reception, with a high collar and a cravat elegantly knotted around his neck. There is always a bunch of roses set into its cold hand, mysteriously replaced before they wither. Some say it's the wardens who mischievously place it here to perpetuate a romantic mystery, others that a woman in black has been seen, but that it never is the same face underneath the dark veil.

The statue represents Heinrich Von S****, a journalist who was famous for his sexual appetite and who boasted more than a thousand conquests. He died in 1889, supposedly poisoned by a jealous rival, who had mixed some arsenic in his champagne during a soirée.

The finger of the statue is shiny, compared to the rest of the body. Women who desire a child, a lover or a more potent husband come to touch it for good luck. The statue also has the reputation of hosting Heinrich's ghost, who manifests himself if he finds a woman—some say any woman—to his liking. But one should never accept his invitation, as you will be found dead in the morning. According to the legend, a letter is always found next to the unfortunate victim's body, accusing Heinrich Von S**** of heartlessness. You die of a broken heart, literally.

I had heard about the legend, or actually seen a documentary about it on some television channel, and, as I was on a professional visit to Vienna, decided to go pay a visit to the statue. It was a beautiful day in May, and the statue was easy enough to find, standing erect, if I may say so, in the middle of a cluster of small mausoleums and tombstones. Looking at the bronze figure, I was surprised by the beauty of his face and the softness of his traits. Could this be the monster of the legend? He looked fragile and sensitive, maybe a little too-well dressed, but then again, he was supposed to go out. He did indeed hold a bunch of red roses, who spread their heady smell around.

I bent slightly to take a whiff, when I noticed the shiny finger. Looking around to see if anybody was nearby as I thought about touching it. My love life hadn't been so great lately, and a new adventure would be welcome. As my hand grabbed the finger, a dark cloud passed in front of the warm spring sun, and a coldness suddenly took hold of my shoulders. As I shivered, I distinctly smelled a delightful cologne and heard a soft voice whisper in my ear: "Oh my dear, won't you invite me for dinner?"

I did actually scream and ran away, leaving the lonely statue standing there. And I swear I saw, as I turned back one last time to make sure no one had played a dirty trick on me, that his face bore the nastiest smirk I had ever seen on a living man's face.

SD

The Hand Of Glory

One candle
To bring light
In darkness
One finger
To point at the living
And mark the liars
Three fingers
To reach out for the sky
And ask for justice
Two fingers
For each lover
That has two-timed and hurt me
Ten fingers
To count the dead
And not miss any

SD